IT'S **Never** *Just* THE **Food** ...

Recipes, Memories and Funny Stories Of My Grandmother and Me

BY GREGORY GALLERANO

Eileen

Hope you enjoy the book

Eat and cook

and

make memories

www.itsneverjustthefood.com

About the Author

Gregory Gallerano attended The New School of the Performing Arts and began his career as an actor, landing small parts in such films as Last Dragon and Married to the Mob. Later with a number of commercials under his belt, he performed in productions of Damn Yankees, Guys and Dolls, and Sweet Charity. He then began writing screenplays, the first being What a Drag, based on his experience of creating a female impersonator's show. He went on to write Let It Go, which he produced and starred in off-Broadway, and two short films that were well received at festivals. Recently, he co-authored a pilot called Playing It Straight about how a gay man's life changes the day he becomes responsible for raising his brother's children. Greg lives in New Jersey. It's Never Just the Food... is his first cookbook.

Christine Brewer is a professional photographer and has owned her own studio since 1998, specializing in wedding photography. She has photographed several books this being her first cookbook. Recently she has branched out and was the on-set photographer for a short film entitled, "Keepsakes."

I want to thank my mom, my dad, and my grandmother, who we simply called Mamma, for filling my life with such amazing love, incredible respect, and of course all that mouthwatering food. I also want to thank my family and friends who supported me during making of this book.

Published by GLG Productions LLC
PO Box 125, Essex Fells, NJ 07006
www.itsneverjustthefood.com

ISBN-1450512852
LCCN-20120900302

Printed in the USA

Table of Contents

Preface

Preface

My name is Greg, and I want to share with you my wonderful memories of my grandmother (who we called Mamma) and her great recipes, her wonderful advice, and everything she did for me that always made my life so special. I also want to share with you my crazy stories about growing up as an overweight, gay guy and show you how, no matter what insanity was going on in my life, my mom and Mamma, with all of their love, made everything okay. Most of all, I want to share with you the food, the mouthwatering food: the creamy wild mushroom risotto that soothed my wounds from my first rumble—well, sort of a rumble; a stuffed eye round that got me out of a lot of trouble; and a meat and spinach ravioli that turned an embarrassing first Communion experience into a wonderful family dinner. See, it was not just the food but also everything that went along with it—great times, fun times, the times upon which memories are built. Whenever something good happened to someone in my family, we would celebrate with a big Italian dinner. When things were not going so well, we would mourn by having a sumptuous meal. Hell, let's face it, when nothing was going on we ate...and ate and ate. Well, at least I did.

As you will soon learn, I've had a relationship with food all of my life, and, as in all relationships, there have been good times and bad times. The bad times usually consist of my getting on the scale and watching the hand go around and around. Throughout my entire life, I must have lost and gained the same hundred pounds. See, I had a weight problem. Did I say "had"? I love when people say, "I had a weight problem." I mean, just because you lose the weight, the problem no longer exists? Let's face it; if you have food issues in your life, you will always have food issues. The trick is to learn how to live with them. As Weight Watchers says, "portion control." So...after forty-something years, I am just now beginning to deal with my love/hate relationship with food.

But, as I said, it was never just the food. It was everything that went along with it. When we sat down as a family and enjoyed Mamma's wonderful cooking, everything with the world was good. No matter what drama was going on in our lives, Mamma's cooking was our escape. It did not matter if it was a Sunday, someone's birthday, a holiday, or a dinner comprising of leftovers—the food she prepared made everything okay.

All right, I know what you're thinking. It was food, not a magic pill—but think back. In a way, doesn't food always put us in a better mood? It could be chocolate, a great meal, ice cream on the Boardwalk, going out to a nice restaurant, having friends over, or just the comfort of a good meal. It's the food and everything that goes along with it that makes us happy.

As for the recipes, times have changed and so should the recipes—who's eating no carbs, who's counting points, and who's no longer eating meat. Therefore, as people and times change, some of Mamma's recipes must be amended. If traditionally healthy but not diet dishes are what you crave, then follow Mamma's original recipes; but if God has cursed you, as he did me, with a metabolism that is slower than a snail's pace, then follow my "reduced fat" versions. You will be amazed how just changing a few ingredients or methods of preparing can lower the fat content and still have the flavor of Mamma's original recipes. Now you must understand that not all the recipes should or can be changed. Some things should just be enjoyed as one of life's indulgences.

Now, if you're not someone who loves food, then there is no hope for you. I don't understand you. I can't help you. You're probably one of those people who say, "Is it that late? I forgot to eat." I mean who forgets to eat? If you fall into this category, just go return this book; don't bother reading it, go buy another book. But if you love food, then sit back and have fun reading my stories and trying these great recipes. More important, share them with your family and friends. It's never just the food. It's the memories that go along with it.

No Need To Panic,
"Just Don't Button It"

Here I am with my pot of tomato sauce cooking on the stove. The zucchini are fried. I just need to make the zucchini parm and cut the salad greens. Mom is in the dining room setting the table. I hope she's using her china. As I look at the clock, I realize that everyone will be here in an hour. Before I forget, I need to chill the wine. Now you're probably wondering what today could be. Is it my birthday, an anniversary party, or a holiday? No, it's just Sunday. As I start to add the meatballs to the sauce, I can smell how good it's going to be. It's funny. Sometimes when I smell my sauce cooking, I can't help feeling like a kid on Sunday morning or on a holiday. I would wake up every Sunday to the smell of sauce cooking. As I got out of bed, I would start to grin from ear to ear with the anticipation of what the day was going to bring. Food! That's right—incredible homemade food.

I remember this one particular Sunday—it was the day of my first Holy Communion. I had just gotten up when I smelt Mamma's sauce cooking. I could not help myself—I ran down to the kitchen to see what was up. My face lit up to see Mamma standing at the stove, stirring the pot of marinara sauce. Then I saw her homemade ravioli laid out on the table. I was in heaven.

Let me tell you a little about Mamma. She was a five-foot-one, one-hundred-pound power-house. She came from an Old World Italian family, where the boys were formally educated and the women learned all the domestic chores. Mamma had a dream of becoming a pharmacist and working with her dad in his drugstore, but that didn't happen. She married the love of her life, and they had one child, my mother. When my grandfather lost his job during the Depression, they opened a children's clothing store. When my grandfather died, Mamma was only fifty-seven. She continued to run the business alone for twenty years until she retired and moved in with us—one of the happiest days of my life. Even though she had great strength, she also had a soft side and a great sense of humor. And oh what a class act! Mamma never left the house, for any reason, unless she looked her best—gloves, hat, and the most adorable outfits that she made herself. See, not only was she a great cook, but she was also an unbelievable seamstress. The costumes and gowns that she made for me were as good as the ones you see on Broadway. Yes, I said costumes. Did I mention I was an aspiring actor? Who am I kidding? When you're in your forties, "aspiring" means "unemployed." Oh, and the gown thing…I also did "drag," but we'll get to that in a later chapter.

So there was Mamma cooking, and I was standing in the middle of the kitchen salivating over the sauce Mamma was making. She looked over and smiled at me with that wonderful smile of hers! I smiled back. She knew what I wanted. She gave me a taste of the sauce. This was something I always did when Mamma was cooking. She never denied me my taste. After that she told me to go upstairs and to get ready for my big day.

I showered and started to get dressed, and that's when it happened. I stood in front of the mirror in complete horror. My First Communion suit was tight; and when I say "tight," I mean TIGHT. When I buttoned the jacket, I looked like a stuffed sausage. I didn't get it. It fit last week. Could three dishes of pasta make a difference? How could I walk into church looking like this? I could feel the sweat start dripping down my face. What should I do? Should I play sick? No. Then I would have to be sick all day, and Mamma was making one hell of a dinner. There I was, looking in the mirror and panicking because the jacket was too tight. I unbuttoned it. Just then Mamma came to see if I was ready. She immediately saw the panic on my face. She asked me why I looked so nervous, but I was too embarrassed to tell her. I just kind of shrugged my shoulders. She walked over and started to fix my tie and to tell me that today would be no big deal. I just had to get up there and say a few prayers, and before I knew it, we would be home having dinner. She smiled and said, "I made your favorite." For a moment the panic was gone. All I could think about was Mamma had made my favorite dish for my First Communion celebration—meat-filled ravioli. Now these were not just any meat ravioli—these were made with five different meats, spinach, and cheese, wrapped in the most amazing light dough. Eating them was bliss. When there was a celebration and it was my turn to choose the menu, I chose these ravioli. Even though they took days to make (these ravioli were small and we ate hundreds of them), Mamma never complained. The thought of the ravioli put a smile on my face. I looked in the mirror and saw a thin, handsome boy. The mind can play such tricks. I took a deep breath and buttoned my jacket. I was ready for my big day. That was until my sister walked by and said, "Boy, that jacket looks tight on you." Great! I could feel the sweat dripping down my face again. I was in full panic mode. Let's just say I knew what panic attacks were at a very young age. It started in school. I'd be in gym, hanging out with my friends thinking how cool I was, when the teacher would announce we were going to split up into teams, shirts vs. skins. I had man boobs at a very young age. Do I need to say anything else? Anyway, Mamma figured out what was wrong and came over to me. She unbuttoned the jacket and said, "Don't worry, just leave it unbuttoned and it will look fine." Could it be that easy? Was that it? Just don't button it. Of course, just don't button it. What a fool I was. It was that simple. Just don't button it. That was Mamma. You never saw her sweat. I am sure she did, but she never let you know. I always felt safe with Mamma.

Just don't button it. All the way to church I kept hearing, "Just don't button it." When we got there, I was feeling great, because—you got it—I just didn't button it.

As we lined up to walk down the aisle, I saw my family sitting in the pew looking very happy. We were just about to start when I saw Sister Martha start walking towards me. She pointed her finger at my jacket. At that moment, all I could feel was my heart pounding. Sister Margaret continued walking towards me. Walking? I mean stomping towards me shaking her big finger at me—all in slow motion. I can still hear her voice in a booming echo. BUTTON YOUR JACKET…NOW. I froze. I started to think how I could get out of this. I scanned the exits. One on the right. Another in the back. Could I make it? But if I split, would they cancel my dinner? Was I willing to take that chance? We were talking about homemade ravioli. I took a deep breath and buttoned the jacket. Sister Margaret took one look at how tight the jacket was and smiled, telling me to just keep it open. I was so embarrassed. I started walking down the aisle all depressed, when I saw my Mamma sitting there. She smiled and mouthed, "I love you." She grabbed my mom's hand, and the two of them looked at me with such pride. Then I saw my dad and the rest of the family. They were all there for me, and at that moment I felt very loved. That day, at the dinner table, we all joked about it. My sister was imitating Sister Martha. My brother was laughing so hard I thought he was going to choke. Everyone was laughing, which was okay with me, because no matter what happened that day, I was sitting with my family. More important, I was sitting with a dish of my Mamma's ravioli in front of me.

Mamma's Marinara Sauce
(a simple sauce for rich ravioli)

Ingredients:
4 cloves of garlic
½ cup olive oil
3 cans (28-ounce size) whole tomatoes
½ cup chopped fresh basil
Salt
2 teaspoons of baking soda
1 6-ounce can tomato paste

Sauté whole garlic cloves slowly in olive oil over medium heat until golden brown. Remove from heat and let cool. In a bowl crush the whole tomatoes with your hands. Put pot back on medium heat and add tomatoes slowly to the oil. Cook for 10 minutes or until bubbling. Add basil, salt, and baking soda. The baking soda is used to blunt the acidity of the tomatoes. Add paste and 3 cups of water. Simmer for about an hour. Yields 12 to 13 cups of sauce.

Greg's Reduced-Fat Marinara Sauce
Only use 2 tablespoons of olive oil, and spray olive oil Pam in the pot when sautéing garlic. Make sure you spray Pam before putting pot on heat.

Mamma's Pasta Dough for Ravioli

Ingredients:
6 cups of all-purpose flour, plus extra for flouring hands and board
½ teaspoon of salt
4 eggs plus 1 yolk
3 tablespoons oil
Water for stiff dough

Sift flour with salt onto a large pastry board to form a mound. Make a well in the mound, leaving some flour at the bottom of the well. Add the eggs and the egg yolk into the center of the well, add the oil, and scramble lightly with a fork. With your hands, gradually pull flour in from the sides. Keep pushing up the flour on the outer wall of the well to keep the sides from breaking. The eggs will absorb the flour, forming a sticky dough. At this time begin to add the water slowly, a little at a time, to form a stiff dough. Sprinkle the board with flour and knead for 10 minutes. Don't let the dough get dry. If it starts to appear too dry, slowly add drops of water to soften. The dough should be elastic but not sticky. As you knead, the dough will stick to your hands. Scrape your fingers and dust with a little flour before you start kneading again. When you are through kneading, the dough should be soft, smooth, and elastic. Cover the dough with wax paper or an inverted bowl and let it stand for about an hour. Yields 300 ravioli.

Note: For healthier dough, try substituting whole wheat flour for regular white flour.

Mamma's Meat Ravioli Filling

Ingredients:
1 stick butter
1 tablespoon olive oil
¼ pound cubed lamb
½ pound cubed pork
3 breasts of chicken, cubed
½ pound lean cubed beef
½ pound cubed veal
2 boxes of frozen chopped spinach (thawed, with all the water squeezed out)
1 cup white wine
2 (8-ounce) packages of cream cheese at room temperature
2 cups Parmigiano Reggiano
2 eggs
2 teaspoons nutmeg
Salt and pepper

In a large pot, melt butter with oil. Add all cubed meat and brown for about 8 minutes. Add drained spinach and white wine and cook for an additional 10 minutes. Set aside to cool.

When the meat and spinach mixture is cooled, it needs to be ground fine. To do this, put it through your meat grinder twice, the first time using the coarse grinding plate and the second time using the fine grinding plate. (The Kitchen Aid has a food grinder attachment. Most grinders come with 6-mille and 8-mille grinding plates.) Now you are ready to add the rest of the ingredients. Stir in the cream cheese, Parmigiano Reggiano cheese, eggs, nutmeg, salt and pepper. Stir until completely smooth and well mixed. There should be no streaks of cream cheese in the mixture. Yields enough filling for 300 ravioli.

Greg's Reduced-Fat Meat Ravioli Filling

Ingredients:
1 stick margarine or reduced-fat margarine
1 tablespoon olive oil
¼ pound cubed lamb
½ pound cubed pork
3 breasts of chicken, cubed
½ pound lean cubed beef
½ pound cubed veal
Salt and pepper
2 boxes of frozen chopped spinach (thawed, with all the water squeezed out)
2 (8-ounce) packages of low-fat cream cheese at room temperature
2 cups low-fat Parmigiano Reggiano
2 teaspoons nutmeg
1 cup white wine
2 eggs

Continue with same cooking directions of Mamma's version of the filling.

How to Make the Ravioli

Cut the dough in half. Cover one half with wax paper and place in a bowl to keep from drying out. Place the other half on your pastry board that has been well floured to prevent sticking. Roll dough into a circle 1/16th of an inch thick—no thicker than that. Work as quickly as possible, so it does not dry out. Gently fold the circle of dough in half to mark the diameter of the circle. Open it up again. Put little mounds of the ravioli filling on one half of the circle and spread evenly with a spatula to about 1/8-inch thickness. Leave a ½-inch border at the edges. Now take the clean half of the dough and fold it over evenly on top of the filled half. If you misjudged and the top half does not meet the edges exactly, gently stretch it a little. If the dough should tear, slightly moisten it with your fingers and gently work it back in place. Sprinkle the top with flour and firmly roll across it with your ravioli rolling pin, making little square imprints. Using your ravioli cutting wheel, firmly press along the grooves to cut the ravioli.

Transfer the ravioli to a tablecloth that has been dusted with semolina, using your dough scraper or a large spatula. Let the ravioli dry for about a half hour or more if necessary. When they are thoroughly dry, place them in rectangular plastic containers that have been lined with wax paper which has been sprinkled with semolina. Sprinkle top of ravioli with semolina and cover with a sheet of wax paper. You can make layers by repeating the process. Freeze the ravioli (they freeze well). When you are ready to cook them, slip out the wax paper sheets and throw the frozen ravioli into rapidly boiling water. It's all right if the semolina gets thrown in the water, too. Cover the pot to bring the water to a boil, stirring occasionally, ever so gently, to be sure the ravioli are not sticking together. When the ravioli are cooked, very gently, as quickly as possible, remove them from the water with a handled strainer and place in a large bowl or platter and cover with tomato sauce. (I prefer spreading them out on a large platter.) Serve immediately with additional tomato sauce and Parmigiano Reggiano cheese brought to the table.

Mamma's Meat Ravioli

Who Cares If You Win or Lose.
It's All About How You Look

My mom always wanted me to have a versatile childhood. She wanted me to take part in everything: Cub Scouts (my mom was the den mother), Webelos (my dad was the leader), and, of course, sports. I was happy going to Skip Randal's Dance School and learning tap and jazz. Yes, even at that age, I knew I was Broadway bound—"the smell of the greasepaint, the roar of the crowd." As you can see, theater was my life. Could I be any more gay? Mom wanted me to play baseball and basketball. So, there I was, an overweight gay kid trying to do sports—not a pretty sight. Mom had no clue, but I love her for trying. First, you should know that I was blessed with the greatest mom anyone could have. How could she not be? She was Mamma's daughter. She is not only my mom, but also my best friend. I know—if you speak to any gay man, he either has the world's greatest mom or a wire-hanger-carrying Joan Crawford mom. My mother was one of the good guys. All she ever really wanted was to be a wife and mother. Now, she won't admit it, but I know I'm her favorite—not so much "favorite", but we have the most in common.

I can still remember one humiliating time when it came to sports, second only to the "shirt vs. skins" experience. It happened when I was on my Cub Scout baseball team. I was about seven. At that age, you are still friends with everyone—not like the middle school, where everyone tries to get into the popular groups and forgets all their childhood geeky friends. I was best friends with two of the school's best athletes, Jake and Tim. Jake was the all-around great-at-everything guy. God smiled on him and gave him brains, looks, athletic talents, and a great personality. Tim was smart and, I guess, cute; but his overbearing mom bought him into his popularity. It was the night before the opening game. We were playing our archrival, Troop 11. We met at the coach's house to get our baseball tee shirts—a gray cotton tee shirt with "Troop 9" in big black letters. The coach passed them out, and everyone tried them on. I ran to the bathroom, pretending I had to pee, and tried it on there. (You know—man boobs.) It didn't fit. I looked at the tag—large. Why did they order me a large? I'm an X-large. You can see I'm an X-large. It must not be mine. I came out and went to my mom, who was one step ahead of me. Everyone ordered two shirts in case one got ripped. She was holding the other one. "Didn't fit?" she whispered in my ear. I just looked at her. "They didn't come in X-large," she again whispered. She could see me starting to sweat. She smiled and through her teeth told me not to panic—we would deal with this when we got home. She looked at her watch, pretending we had to leave, and we split. Oh boy! Did we deal with it at home! As I walked in the door, I was still screaming that my life was over. My mother was still trying to calm me down. Mamma was at the kitchen table, cutting up zucchini. She told me she couldn't wait to come to my first game. I told her in my overdramatic voice, "Victoria Paige will not dance the dance of the red shoes tomorrow." (I had just seen The Red Shoes on the four thirty movie last week.) She smiled and said, "I hope that's not true. I'm making ratatouille, so we can have it for dinner after the game." For a second I forgot what was wrong. I asked her if she was making polenta to go with it. "Is there any other way?" she asked. I sat down and started to help her cut the vegetables. For a moment, all was well. Then my mom sat down and threw the two shirts on the chair. When I saw them, it all came back, and I started to panic. I screamed that I was quitting the team. Mamma asked what was the problem. My mom explained that the shirt didn't fit. Mamma saw there were two shirts and immediately had the solution. She grabbed the shirts and told me to follow her. A few measurements, Mamma staying up all night, and I had a shirt that fit. It was amazing work. You would never have known that she took two shirts that didn't fit and made them into one that did fit. That next day, at the field, I felt like nothing could stop me. It was going to be a great season!

That feeling evaporated on the ride home from the game. My friend Tim's mom was driving. The mothers took turns staying after the game, giving the coach time to talk to us. Tim's mom was bitching the entire way home because we had lost the game. Jake and Tim were in the back seat moping, visually upset about the loss. I was glancing out the window, thinking about my Mamma's ratatouille and how good it was going to be served over her creamy polenta. I could taste it. I was really getting into my food daydream when I heard Tim's mom yelling out my name. "Greg, did you hear me?" I suddenly snapped out of my ratatouille fantasy. She was asking me if I thought it was fair. I asked her if what was fair. She said about Jake not pinch-hitting for Allan. I then realized she was still complaining about how the coach should have let Jake bat out of turn so we could win the game. You see, our coach was extremely fair. He felt that everyone should have a chance to play in every game and to get a turn to bat, and Allan had not batted yet. Allan was a skinny nerd who wanted to be on the team less than I did. Now, I wish I could tell you that Allan at least hit the ball; but this is not an Afterschool Special. You remember—those "Sara T., Portrait of a Teenage Alcoholic" or "Dawn, Portrait of a Teenage Runaway." Mine would have been "Greg, Portrait of a Teenage Overeater." Back to the car: Tim's mom was still ranting, saying, "I know you guys are very upset about this." She looked right at me, noticing I couldn't give a shit, and said, "Well, most of you. Greg, you pretend someone in one of your Broadway musicals screwed up, and the show could not go on. Then you will understand how we feel." No way! Was I just read by my friend's mom? Note: Those of you reading this who are not gay, have no gay friends, or have never seen Will and Grace, to "read" people means to put them in their place by telling them exactly what you think of them. I wanted to turn around and say, "Bitch, that's what understudies are for." But I was only a kid, so I just smiled in embarrassment. That night I was sitting at the table, eating my ratatouille over polenta, and I thought about what Tim's mom had said. Why didn't I care about losing the game? At that moment I looked over at Mamma. She looked at me and said, "Sorry you lost, but you looked good out there in your shirt." I smiled and thought, "She's right—I did." I mean, who cares if you win or lose? I was gay. It's always about how you look.

Ratatouille Served Over Polenta

Ratatouille

Ingredients:
6 medium zucchini
6 medium fryer peppers (Light green about 6-7" long and about 3" wide)
1 large eggplant
1 (28-ounce) can of plum tomatoes
Olive Oil Pam spray
2 teaspoons olive oil
2 cloves elephant garlic, finely chopped
1 medium onion, coarsely chopped
3 heaping teaspoons of tomato paste
1 teaspoon of salt, or season to taste

Select firm zucchini, wash, and scrape lightly. Remove the top of the zucchini and cut a thin slice from the bottom and discard. Cut in half and cut each half lengthwise. Remove the seedy center of the zucchini as this tends to get mushy. Slice the zucchini crosswise, about ¼-inch thick. The cut pieces will be crescent-shaped.

Wash fryer peppers, cut in half, and remove stem and seeds. Cut the halves into quarters lengthwise, and cut each quarter in half crosswise.

Wash the eggplant; remove top and a slice from bottom. Cut in quarters and clean out some of the seeds. Cut the eggplant in 1-inch chunks.

Drain the juice from the can of plum tomatoes into a bowl and set aside. Hand crush the plum tomatoes, removing the inside stem if you desire, and set aside.

Spray a 5- or 7-quart pot with Olive Oil Pam spray, add the 2 teaspoons of olive oil, and sauté the garlic over medium heat for 1 minute. Add onions and sauté until translucent (about 4 minutes). If the garlic and onions stick to the bottom of the pot, turn off the heat and spray the mixture with the Olive Oil Pam spray, then continue sautéing. Mix in the tomato paste, melting it into the mixture, about 2 minutes, stirring constantly. Stir in the juice from the can of plum tomatoes and add the hand-crushed plum tomatoes. Season with 1 teaspoon of salt or season to taste. Cook for 5 minutes. Add peppers, zucchini, and eggplant. Coat all vegetables with the tomato, onion, and garlic mixture. Simmer, stirring often, until vegetables are tender (about 10 to 15 minutes). Serve over polenta. Serves 6 to 8.

Note: If you would like to add protein to the ratatouille, add a 1-pound can of cannellini beans with the liquid, and reduce the juice from the plum tomatoes to half.

Polenta

Ingredients:
3 cups water
1 cup yellow cornmeal
1 cup cold water
1 tablespoon of light margarine
Salt to taste
Bring the 3 cups of water to a boil. Combine the cornmeal with the cold water, stirring to break up any lumps. Add this gradually to the boiling water, stirring constantly. Add the margarine and salt and continue cooking for 20 minutes, stirring constantly. Pour polenta into an oval vegetable dish and let stand at room temperature until ready to use. When ready, turn polenta onto a platter and slice. Serve the ratatouille over the polenta. Serves 6 to 8.

Ratatouille Served Over Polenta

It's a Rumble,
So Just Shuffle Ball Change Step Hop

So, as you can see, sports were not my thing. Now cooking, watching movies, and musicals—those were things I loved. What "loved"? I still to this day love cooking and musicals. In fact, before I started school, I always watched my favorite TV show, The Galloping Gourmet. Remember him? He used to open a bottle of wine in the beginning of the show; and by the end of the show, he would be hammered. I would take my mom's pots and pans and use my play dough as food, pretending to make the same dishes he was preparing. I used to have a blast. I probably got my love of cooking from watching my Mamma cook all those fabulous meals.

Then there was my other passion. I love Broadway shows and movies—especially musicals. I know a lot about musicals, because not only am I gay and it's in my DNA, but also because my mom made sure I saw all the old great ones. It started when I was about eight years old. My mom would wake me up around 11:15 p.m., just in time for the late movie. I saw some of the best: Singing in the Rain (my favorite of all movies), The Harvey Girls, Meet Me in St Louis, A Star is Born. Big surprise! I was a Judy fan.

I remember this one particular Sunday. We had just finished a big Sunday dinner. I was helping my mom and my grandmother put the leftovers away. What I really was doing was hiding the leftover risotto so no one would eat it. I know—I had just finished dinner, and I was already worried that someone was going to eat the leftover risotto. I told you—food issues—but if you had tasted my grandmother's risotto, you would understand. Later that night, we were all sitting around the TV waiting for the Sunday Night Movie to start. Usually, it was some action flick or romantic comedy; but that night it was "West Side Story." I had already seen it a year ago in the movie theater with my mom. (It was a re-release. How old do you think I am?) It was a big deal when a movie aired on network TV for the first time. Remember, way back then there was no cable and no video. The only time you saw a movie on television was when the network aired it. My entire family was looking forward to this movie.

The next day at school everyone was talking about what they did over the weekend, and I was shocked at how many boys watched West Side Story. Some of the boys were saying the Jets would have killed the Sharks. Other boys were saying the Sharks would have definitely creamed the Jets. Then I heard it. Chris, the most popular kid in our school, said we should play "rumble" after school instead of "war." We could do Jets vs. Sharks. Finally! A game I wanted to play. I mean who the hell wants to play "war"? Really, you spend your youth pretending you're in a war; then when you're of age, you shit bricks that you might have to go to war. My mom always pushed me to get involved in afternoon activities, and the " 'West Side Story' Rumble" was exactly my type of game. I walked up to Chris and said, "Hey, I have a really big backyard. Why don't we meet at my house, and we can have the rumble there?" Everyone agreed, and so it was—my house at 3:15, Jets against Sharks. I could hear the overture in my head. I couldn't wait for the school day to end. You see, I never really had a lot in common with the other guys in my class. We got along and hung out, but I never cared for the same things that they liked—mainly sports. I was so excited that we were finally into the same thing—a musical! How great was that? I always felt like an oddball because of the way I felt about musicals. The bell rang—it was "rumble" time! On my way home, I thought about which team I wanted to be on—the Sharks or the Jets? I ran into the house and told my mom that everyone was coming over to do "West Side Story." God bless my mom. She asked no questions. She just smiled and said, "I'll make snacks." We met in my backyard, which was large and wooded. Chris started to direct, telling everyone to get fake weapons. Fine, he could direct; but I was doing the choreography. Everyone picked up sticks, and some of the kids had brought fake knives. Chris assigned teams, and I was a Jet. When the teams were set, Chris told us it was time to "rumble." I yelled, "Wait! Don't we have to go over the steps?" They all looked at me, puzzled. "You know," I continued, "shuffle ball change, step, hop." I demonstrated, ending in this grand leap. They all just stood there in utter amazement, and it was not because they were impressed with my leap. Then they laughed and told me to stop joking. Everyone started pretending to stab each other. It was appalling!! No one was leaping or fan kicking! They just ran around—Jerome Robbins would have died. (He was the choreographer.) I was so pissed that I picked up a stick and angrily joined in the pretend stabbing war. Kids were falling down, pretending to be dead. I mean literally falling. No one spun, pirouetted, or even leaped. I was so depressed. That night, I sat in my room alone—just me and my "West Side Story" album. My mom and Mamma came in to check on me. They both wore a silly smile. Mamma told me that they had heard the performance in the yard did not go well. We all started to laugh. Next thing I know, all three of us were downstairs listening to the album and snacking on, you guessed it, the leftover risotto. After our snack, I showed them the way it should have been done, twirling around the room and leaping through the air. Mamma and Mom just watched and applauded. I often make Mamma's risotto—sometimes her way and sometimes my vegetarian low-fat way. Either way, whenever I do make it, I always think of the time that my mom and Mamma made me feel like one of the Jets.

Mamma's Mushroom Risotto

Ingredients:
12 tablespoons of butter
½ cup chopped porcini mushrooms
½ cup chopped portobello mushrooms
½ cup shiitake mushrooms
½ cup white mushrooms
1 medium onion, chopped fine
2 cups of long grain rice (I use Uncle Ben's)
2 quarts of chicken broth (you can use home made chicken soup)–see page 60
1 tablespoon of powdered saffron dissolved in 2 tablespoons of broth
1 cup of grated Parmigiano Reggiano cheese
Plus additional grated cheese for garnishing.

Melt 8 tablespoons of butter in saucepan. Wash mushrooms and squeeze until all the water is out. Add mushrooms to the pan and brown. Remove the mushrooms and set aside. Brown onion, then add rice and brown for a second or two. Reduce the heat to medium. Add broth about ½ cup at a time, stirring constantly. Do not let the rice become too dry. Cook 40 to 45 minutes over flame, stirring constantly. Taste for tenderness (should be "al dente.") When the rice has reached the desired tenderness, add the saffron and mix well. Add the mushrooms and stir to distribute evenly in rice. Add remaining 4 tablespoons of butter and the Parmigiano cheese, cover, and let stand 10 minutes. Sprinkle with Parmigiano cheese and serve. Serves 8.

If "al dente" rice is not cooked enough for your taste, use an additional ½ cup to 1 cup of broth for softer rice. The rice should not be mushy. The rice grains should appear separated. This is the conventional way to prepare risotto.

Mamma's Mushroom Risotto

Greg's Brown Rice Vegetarian Reduced-Fat Risotto

Ingredients:
Substitute brown rice for white rice.
Substiute 8 tablespoons of low-fat margarine instead of the 12 tablespoons butter. No need to add margarine at the end of recipe.
Substitute 2½ quarts of vegetarian broth instead of 2 quarts of chicken broth,
Substitute reduced-fat Parmigiano Reggiano cheese for reguler grated cheese.

Continue with same directions as original recipe.

Note: You may substitute any vegetables for the mushrooms.

The Perfect Dish for a Pot Party

When I started junior high, I was about 70 pounds overweight. I knew by the third day that if I did not do something, this was going to be three years of complete hell and total humiliation. Think about it—fat and gay. I was a bully's wet dream, so I came up with a plan. I avoided "complete hell" by making friends with all the popular girls, who were, of course, dating the popular guys. This would ensure that none of the guys would bother me, because I was friendly with their girlfriends. It worked so well that I actually became friends with some of the guys. As for the "total humiliation," that was a different story, which I will tell you about right now. Well, Lori Chiccolinni, one of the most popular girls in school, got me invited to her best friend's (Kelly's) party. I think the main reason she was so popular was that she was fully developed by seventh grade. When I first met her, I asked her to help me find my class, thinking she was one of the teachers. She thought that was so cute. Of course, only the most popular kids were invited to Kelly's party; and, yes, I was included on that list. The night before the party, I was helping my mom and Mamma with the dishes. I told them about the party, and they were so glad that I had made new friends. Mamma asked me what I wanted to bring to the party. See, my mom and Mamma always taught us to never arrive at a dinner or a party empty-handed. I told her that I had not really given it any thought. Whatever she decided would be fine. We chose to make her tortellini salad. This mouthwatering dish was made with tortellini, pieces of provolone cheese, sopressata, pepperoni, prosciutto, olives, roasted peppers, and all kinds of other good stuff. These ingredients were all tossed together in a seasoned olive oil. My mouth is watering just thinking about it. The next day my dad took me out to buy a new pair of Jordins—they were the big and tall version of Jordache jeans. When we returned, we found my mom, sister, and Mamma around the kitchen table. They were having a great time cutting vegetables and dicing pieces of provolone and sopressata. I looked at them, so different in one way and so alike in others. Three generations sitting there laughing and enjoying being together. That's what Mamma loved most about food: whether we were cooking it or eating it, food always brought us together.

As soon as they saw me, they begged me to try on my new jeans. Yeah, like they had to beg! I came downstairs and modeled my new jeans for everyone. They told me how great I looked. I was ready for the party: me, my new jeans, and Mamma's pasta salad. Mom drove me to the party and wanted to wait until I got in the house, but I told her I was in junior high and I did not need my mom. I thought I was so cool. I waited until my mom pulled away, and then I rang the doorbell. Kelly answered the door, and she just kind of giggled and gave me a hug when she saw me with a covered bowl. She asked me what I was carrying. I told her I had brought my grandmother's famous tortellini salad and asked if I should put it on the food table. She just smiled at me. At that second the phone rang, and Kelly ran to answer it, directing me over her shoulder to go to the basement and join the others. When I got down there, the first thing I did was look for Lori. All I could see was a light layer of smoke. Everyone was just hanging around listening to music. It wasn't my much-loved disco, as sung by Donna Summer, but hard rock, as played and sung by Skynard and Zeppelin. There I was, just me and my pasta salad, and everyone was staring at me. As I walked around, I noticed that most of the people were either drinking or smoking pot. It was the first time I had ever smelled or seen pot. You have to understand, I was a "Polly Purebred." I lived a very sheltered life. As Adam Ant would say, "Don't drink. Don't smoke. What do you do?" I'll tell you what I did. I ate. While I was standing there in pure fright, one of the guys came over and asked me what I had. I told him it was a pasta salad. He smiled and said, "Cool." Then he offered me a toke. I just shook my head indicating a "no thanks." Then he took my pasta salad. All I could think of was that I had to get my mom's Tupperware back. Kelly came over and grabbed me, telling me not do anything I didn't want to do. Then she told me there was beer, if I wanted any. I just smiled, but I could feel a panic attack creeping up. I asked myself, "Where the hell is Lori?" I knew she wasn't anything like the others. She would never act like that. Right on cue, Lori came out from under the table, fixing her shirt. Her boyfriend, Brian, was right behind her. That was it! I got so freaked out that I called my mom to pick me up.

I still serve Mamma's tortellini salad and bring it to parties. Whenever I do, my friends and I laugh about the time a fat gay boy brought a tortellini salad to a pot party.

Mamma's Tortellini Salad

Ingredients:
3 (8-ounce) bags of spinach and cheese tortellini
1 cup cubed provolone cheese
1 cup cubed sopressata
½ cup cubed pepperoni.
½ cup prosciutto,
½ cup sliced green olives
½ cup sliced black olives
1 cup sliced vinegar peppers
½ cup chopped artichoke hearts
½ cup chopped sun-dried tomatoes with the oil from the jar

In a large pot, boil tortellini for 5 minutes less than the package directs. You want the tortellini to be al dente (not fully cooked). Drain and let cool. In a large bowl, add the rest of the ingredients. Toss the cooled tortellini into the bowl. Toss with dressing and chill until served.

Mamma's Italian Dressing

Ingredients:
2 cloves chopped garlic
1 teaspoon onion powder
2 teaspoons dried oregano
½ teaspoon ground black pepper
½ teaspoon dried basil
1 teaspoon dried parsley
2 teaspoon salt
1 teaspoon pepper
¼ cup red wine vinegar (you can use balsamic or white)
1 cup olive oil
2 tablespoons water

In a small bowl mix together all dry ingredients. Whisk together vinegar, oil and water, slowly adding dry ingredients.

Note: For a lower-fat dressing, just use less oil and more vinegar, or, if it has too heavy a vinegar taste, use less oil and add water.

Greg's Shrimp Reduced-Fat Tortellini Salad

Ingredients:
3 (8-ounce) bags of spinach and cheese tortellini
2 pounds medium boiled shrimp, fresh or frozen
½ cup sliced green olives
½ cup sliced black olives
1 cup sliced vinegar peppers
½ cup chopped artichoke hearts
½ cup chopped sun-dried tomatoes, drained of oil

In a large pot, boil tortellini for 5 minutes less than the package directs. You want the tortellini to be al dente (not fully cooked). Drain and let cool. In a large bowl, add the rest of the ingredients. Toss the cooled tortellini into the bowl. Toss with dressing and chill until served.

Tortellini Salads

Who Puts an Italian Restaurant Next to a Fat Camp?

Ragu! Pasta with ragu sauce was my favorite Sunday dinner. Now there are many different types of sauces, such as marinara or tomato and basil Bolognese; but my favorite was ragu. Not only was pasta with ragu my favorite, but it was our most traditional Sunday dinner. Ragu was a very rich sauce made with several meats. Even the smell was rich. It was made with pork bones, braciola (pounded pork, veal, or beef rolled with garlic and cheese and cooked in the sauce) and Mamma's great fried meatballs. (That's if the meatballs made it into the sauce.) We would grab the freshly fried ones and eat them before she even had a chance to add them to the sauce. This used to make Mamma crazy. I remember, as a kid, how I hated dressing up for dinner every Sunday. All my friends would get to go to the movies or hang out, but not us. We would have to stay in our church clothes all day and be at home. If it were not for the food, I think I would have killed myself. You know, it's true what they say—you don't miss something until it's no longer there. I never got that until the summer I went to "fat camp." Yes, I did say "fat camp." It was the summer before my first year of high school. My parents will tell you that we made the decision together. I'm telling you that I had no say in the matter. I was sent to "fat camp" like a prisoner! My crime—overeating!

The camp was located in upstate New York, and, get this, it was located right next to an Italian restaurant. When the wind blew a certain way, the smell of Italian food permeated the air. You had to see all of us fat kids. We were doing our calisthenics when all of a sudden a breeze would blow our way. We would all stop what we were doing and just inhale the smell of pizza or veal Parmesan. We looked like a bunch of zombies in a trance. And yes, we fat kids knew just what the special of the day was by the smell. When it came to smelling food, we were like hound dogs. You would think it would be torturous, but a smell was better than nothing.

The first two weeks of camp were hell. It was like being in the "big house." You needed to learn the ropes—and learn them fast. I remember my first dinner. They were serving chicken. I was in line watching as the food was being dished out. They were giving us only one piece of chicken, half of a baked potato, and steamed string beans. I could feel myself panicking. As I'm standing there waiting my turn, the kid behind me whispered in my ear, "Tell them you're allergic to dark meat." I just looked at him. "What?" I asked. Again he whispered, "Tell them you're allergic to dark meat." I continued to look at him. He then said, "The breast is bigger than the thigh." I quickly made an assessment of both pieces, and he was right. Leave it to a fat guy to be so clever when it comes to his meals. So when it was my turn, I told them I was allergic to dark meat, and from that day on, I became a breast man. Well, when it came to chicken, that is. Bob—that was the kid's name—became my best friend. He knew all the ins and outs. This was his third sentence. He knew who had the candy stash, which counselor could be bribed—all the good stuff you had to know to make it. I know I'm being a little melodramatic, but it was hard. Think about it. First they took us out of our homes. For most of us it was our first time away from our families. Then they took away the one thing that would make us feel better—our food. Then, to top it all off, they made us do the one thing we hated—exercise.

One Sunday was particularly bad. A group of us were getting ready to take a nature walk. They gave us a break on Sundays—no sports. To me a break would have been a couch, a TV, and a bag of Combos. We were just about to leave when the wind shifted and our daily smell of heaven engulfed the air, but this time everyone looked confused. We had never smelled this one before. For the first time no one knew what the special was—but I did. It was the smell of ragu. I started to get so hungry—not so much for pasta with ragu, but for home. I thought about my family and how they were probably sitting around the table, laughing and having a great time. That moment was the first time I realized how important my family was to me and how important Sunday dinners were.

When I got to high school, everyone complimented me about how good I looked. Unfortunately, by graduation I had gained all my weight back. I still had not grasped the portion control thing they tried to teach us at camp. To this day, when I make Mamma's ragu, I can't help remembering that summer when a bunch of fat kids ran around trying to get whiff of "today's special."

Mamma's Ragu

Braciole

Ingredients:
2 pounds flank steak (you can buy them already cut and pounded from your butcher)
4 cloves garlic
½ cup grated Parmigiano Reggiano
½ cup chopped parsley
Salt and pepper

Prepare braciole by pounding the flank steak as thin as possible without breaking meat, then cutting into individual cutlets. Rub the braciole with garlic and sprinkle with cheese, parsley, salt, and pepper. Starting at one short end, roll up steak tightly to enclose the filling completely. Using butcher twine, tie the steak rolls to secure. Set aside to fry. Serves 6 to 8.

NOTE: To make the braciole lower fat, you can use veal or pork instead of the beef. You can also bake the braciole.

Baking Braciole
Place braciole on a Pam-sprayed cookie sheet. Place in a preheated 350 degree oven and bake for 25 minutes.

Mamma's Meatballs

Ingredients:
½ pound of ground pork,
½ pound of ground veal
1 pound of ground beef
2 eggs
1 cup of breadcrumbs
¾ cup grated Parmigiano Reggiano
2 cloves of garlic, minced
Salt and pepper

In a large bowl, mix all ingredients by hand using a light touch. When fully mixed grab a small amount of the mixture and roll into balls about the size of a small egg. Set aside. Serves 6 to 8.

NOTE: To make the meatballs lower fat, you can use veal or turkey instead of the beef. You can also bake the meatballs.

Baking Meatballs

Place meatballs on a Pam-sprayed cookie sheet. Place in a preheated 350-degree oven and bake for 25 minutes.

Mamma's Ragu Sauce

Ingredients:
½ cup olive oil
Meatballs
Rolled braciole
1 pound pork bones or 1 pound of pork meat
3 cloves of garlic
½ cup chopped parsley
3 cans (28-ounce size) whole tomatoes, crushed by hand
1 can (6 ounce size) tomato paste
Salt and pepper

In the olive oil, brown the meatballs and set aside. Then brown the braciole and pork bones (or pork meat) and set aside. Fry garlic and parsley in the olive oil until the garlic is golden brown. Cool slightly, then add the tomatoes and let cook for ½ an hour. Add braciole and pork bones (or pork meat). When tomatoes have cooked ¾ of an hour (or when the oil rises to the surface), add paste and let cook for about 5 or 10 minutes. Gradually add 1 cup of water if needed (if the ragu appears too thick) and let cook for 2 hours, stirring occasionally. One half hour before the ragu is done, add the meatballs. Serves 8 to 10.

NOTE: To make the gravy lower fat, you can also bake the pork or pork bones in the oven at 350-degrees for 25 minutes on a Pam-sprayed cookie sheet. Since there will be no frying the meat, you can cut the olive oil to ¼ cup. Start gravy at "Fry garlic …"

Mamma's Ragu

Yes, I Crocheted a Baby Blanket

I remember a particular Sunday when Deniz (my sister's first born) was only about three months old. My sister was sitting on the couch trying to calm him. She had wrapped him in the blanket I made. Yes, I crocheted a baby blanket. Yes, you read that right. I took a weaving class in high school and was proud of it. I crocheted every time I had a free minute. Now imagine this: I even crocheted at the lunch table with the jocks and their girlfriends. They sat there hanging out while I worked on my blanket. That Sunday my mom and I were in the kitchen, helping Mamma cook. We were making Mamma's chicken rollatini. These are thin chicken breast cutlets rolled with ham, cheese, and parsley. Then they're sautéed in butter and white wine with a touch of rosemary. When you take your first bite, the flavor of the cheese, butter, and hint of rosemary explodes in your mouth. They are amazing-but I digress. The baby was getting louder and very cranky, which was making my sister very nervous. My mom washed her hands and went to help her. Mamma and I just kept rolling the chicken cutlets. My mom tried to quiet the baby but had no luck either. The more the baby cried, the more my sister got nervous. My mom came back to roll and Mamma gave it a shot. As soon as the baby got in Mamma's arms, he just looked at her and smiled. My Mom went over and sat next to my sister, Mamma, and the baby. Then the baby started to giggle. Well! That brought everyone running over to take a look-my brother-in-law, my dad, my brother, and his fiancée. There they were-my entire family around Mamma and our newest family member. Well, almost everyone. I was still in the kitchen up to my armpits in raw chicken; but as I looked at them, I felt a great joy. I realized how blessed I was. We were all together, which always made Mamma happy.

That night during dinner, while everyone was enjoying the chicken, I just could not stop looking at my new nephew. I thought about how lucky he was to be in this family, because no matter how crappy it got out there growing up, he could always come back home to us. Trust me. That thought always got me through the day.

Mamma's Chicken Rollatini

Ingredients:
1 pound chicken cutlets, cut or pounded thin (cut large cutlets in half—size should be approximately 3 inches by 3 inches)
2 cloves of garlic
½ pound of boiled ham, cut in ½-inch strips
½ pound of Swiss cheese, cut in ½-inch strips
½ cup grated Parmigiano Reggiano cheese
½ cup chopped parsley
Salt and pepper
¼ cup of chopped rosemary
4 tablespoons of butter
2 tablespoons of olive oil
½ cup of all-purpose flour
½ cup of white wine

Rub each cutlet lightly with garlic. Add one strip of ham and Swiss cheese. Then sprinkle each cutlet with 2 teaspoons of grated Parmigiano Reggiano cheese and chopped parsley. Add a dash of salt, pepper, and rosemary. Roll each filled cutlet and tie with string, or use toothpicks to hold together.

In a large skillet melt butter and oil. (The olive oil will keep the butter from burning.) Dip each chicken roll in flour, making sure you cover the roll completely. Brown rolls in oil and butter for about 10 minutes, turning frequently. Add ½ cup white wine and let simmer for 8 to 10 minutes more on a low heat, occasionally scraping the bottom of the pan. When serving, untie or take the toothpicks out of the rolls. Arrange on a platter and pour sauce from pan over rolls. Serves 6 (2 rolls per person).

Greg 's Reduced-Fat Chicken Rollatini

Ingredients:
1 pound chicken cutlets, cut or pounded thin (cut large cutlets in half—size should be approximately 3 inches by 3 inches)
2 cloves of garlic
½ pound of low-fat boiled ham, cut in ½-inch strips
½ pound of low-fat Swiss cheese, cut in ½-inch strips
½ cup grated Parmigiano Reggiano cheese
½ cup chopped parsley
Salt and pepper
¼ cup of chopped rosemary
Butter-flavored Pam spray
1 tablespoon of margarine
1 tablespoon of olive oil
½ cup chicken broth
3 tablespoons of all-purpose flour
½ cup white wine

Rub each cutlet lightly with garlic. Add one slice of ham and Swiss cheese. Then sprinkle each cutlet with 2 teaspoons of grated Parmigiano Reggiano cheese and parsley. Add a dash of salt, pepper and rosemary. Roll each filled cutlet and tie with string or use toothpicks to hold together.

Place rolled chicken on a large cookie sheet that has been sprayed with Pam. Bake for 10 minutes at 375 degrees. In a large skillet, melt margarine in oil and chicken broth. Take rolls out of oven and place them in skillet. Sprinkle flour on chicken and then add wine. Let simmer 8 to 10 minutes on a low heat, occasionally scraping the bottom of the pan. When serving, untie or take the toothpicks out of the rolls. Arrange on a platter and pour sauce from pan over rolls. . Serves 6 (2 rolls per person).

Mamma's Chicken Rollatini

I Want My VCR?

"And I Am Telling You I'm Not Going." No, that is not what I used to say to my dates when they tried to break up with me. It is my favorite song from my favorite Broadway show, Dreamgirls. I was obsessed with it. When I was 18, I had seen it at least ten times, and by the end of its run, that number was close to fifty. The show starred the legendary Jennifer Holliday. Of course, I never saw Jennifer in the show. She was always out the days I went to see it. I did get to see her do the number on the Tony Awards. In fact, my best friend, Steven, taped it, so we watched it almost every day. You see, Steven came from a very wealthy family, and they had every new gadget long before anyone else did-microwave, movie camera, and, of course, a VCR. In those days, VCRs were very expensive, and not everyone could afford one, especially my family. I had to go to Steven's house if I wanted to watch the tape, which got tiresome, so I dropped hints to my parents that all I wanted for Christmas was a VCR. My sister kept telling me they were not going to spend that much for just my gift-it was just too expensive. I was convinced that if I played my cards right, I would get it. I started being a perfect "angel" months before Christmas. I came home on time, I never gave anyone lip, and I did everything I was told to do. I was the perfect son.

Christmas Eve finally arrived, and we started opening our gifts from each other. One by one we opened them, but no VCR. I thought my parents were saving it for last. Then my mom opened the last gift, and she and Mamma got up to serve dessert. I yelled out, "Wait! Is that it? Nothing else?" My dad looked at me and said, "That's it." He had no clue what I was talking about. My brother looked at me and said, "You thought you were getting the VCR." My sister just looked at me as if to say, "I told you so." I spoke to no one during dessert, and I went to bed pissed, humiliated, and depressed. Merry Christmas to me.

Christmas Day we all went to church as usual. I was still being a brat and not talking to any-one. When we got back, my mom finished setting the table and Mamma was cooking. She was making her traditional Christmas dinner, homemade manicotti with Bolognese sauce. Her manicotti were "to die for." Mamma made her own dough, and the manicotti were so light they could float away. Everyone waited all year for them, and let me tell you, they were worth the wait.

I went into the kitchen looking for my taste of the Bolognese sauce that was simmering on the stove. I started to spoon some out when I heard it. Mamma told me to stay out of the pot. I stood there in shock. Did I hear right? Was I dreaming? I looked at her and smiled. "Just get-ting a taste," I said. There was no smile. She did not even look up. All she did was wave her hand, tell me I was in the way, and asked me to get out of the kitchen. I felt dizzy, faint. Was this Mamma or some pod person? I walked over, sat down, and asked her what was wrong. She said she did not like the way I was acting over the tape machine. I corrected her and told her it was called a VCR. She was not amused. I started to bitch that it wasn't fair. They knew how much I wanted it. She again snapped at me and told me not to refer to my parents as "they." It was disrespectful. She was not giving me an inch. I asked her if I had been that bad. She looked at me and said, "Yes, and I'm very surprised at you." Her words were like a knife in my heart. I tried to rationalize it by explaining how I did all this good stuff and to what avail? I did not get the VCR, and my Christmas was ruined. She snapped back asking me, "Why? Because you didn't get what you wanted? Listen, be glad you have what you do have. Do nice things because you want to. I don't do all this cooking and preparing in the hope of getting a reward. I do it because I want to do it, because it's important that we are together as a family. Who cares what gifts we get? We get gifts every day—each other." Wow, was I put in my place! I never knew Mamma had it in her. I gave her a big hug and kiss and told her how sorry I was. She smiled and kissed me. Then she told me to go apologize to my parents, which I did.

My dad's family came shortly after that, and before dinner we opened our gifts. We all dug in, and within ten minutes the room was just filled with ripped paper and tossed bows. We were just about finished when my mom told me she had found one more gift from last night that I had forgotten to open. This was it. Leave it to my dad. He wanted me to open it in front of everybody, so they could see my joy. My mom handed me a wrapped gift about the size of a book. I was completely confused. I opened it, and it was a VCR tape. My sister snatched the card and read it aloud. It said, "Now you can watch Jennifer any time you want. Love, Steven." My sister asked, "What did you do? Tell everyone you were getting a VCR?" One of my cousins asked if I had received one. My sister looked at me and started to laugh uncontrollably, saying, "No, but I guess he thought he was." Then she told the whole family about how I had been asking for one all year, and everyone laughed. Then they all started to make jokes. "Let's rent a movie tonight," or, "Hey, Greg, do you have any tapes you want to watch?" I was just about to get all pissed off again, when I caught a glimpse of Mamma. She was in the kitchen getting ready to serve the manicotti. I thought about what Mamma had said about how lucky we all were. I just went along with all the jokes and laughed with everyone. Besides, how could I get pissed? We were just about to sit down to Mamma's manicotti. We still have manicotti every Christmas. When I make them I can't help thinking about that Christmas and how Mamma showed me what the holidays were really about—being with friends and family, sharing good food.

Bolognese Sauce

Ingredients:
½ cup of olive oil
½ cup chopped onions
2 chopped cloves of garlic
½ cup chopped carrots
½ cup chopped celery
½ cup chopped mushrooms
¾ pound chopped ground beef
½ cup chopped parsley
3 cans (28-ounce size) whole tomatoes, crushed by hand
1 can (6-ounce size) tomato paste
½ stick of butter
Salt and pepper to taste

Heat oil in large pot. Sauté onions and garlic until they change color, usually about 3-5 minutes. Add carrots, celery, and mushrooms, and sauté for 5 more minutes. Add ground beef and parsley, and sauté for 10 more minutes or until meat starts to brown. Add tomatoes, salt, pepper, and let cook for 10 minutes on a medium flame. Add tomato paste and simmer on a low heat for 30 minutes more. When sauce is finished, add the butter. Mix and serve. Yields 12 cups

Note: To make it reduced fat, just substitute veal or turkey for the beef. Cut oil to ¼ cup and eliminate the butter.

Mamma's Manicotti

Dough

Ingredients:
3 cups of all-purpose flour, plus extra for flouring hands and board
½ teaspoon of salt
2 eggs
1 tablespoon olive oil
½ cup of warm water

Sift flour with salt onto a large pastry board to form a hill, and make a well in the center, leaving some flour at the bottom of the well. Break the eggs into the center, add the oil, and scramble with a fork. With your hands, gradually pull flour in from the sides. Keep pushing up the flour on the outer wall of the well to keep the sides from breaking. The eggs will absorb the flour, forming sticky dough; at this time begin to add the water slowly, a little at a time, to form stiff dough. Sprinkle the board with flour and knead for 10 minutes. Don't let the dough get dry. If it starts to appear too dry, slowly add drops of water to soften. The dough should be elastic but not sticky. As you knead, the dough will stick to your hands. Scrape your fingers and dust with a little flour before you start kneading again. Knead for about 10 minutes. Cover the dough and let it stand for 15 minutes.

Filling

Ingredients:
1 pound of ricotta cheese
2 eggs
2 ounces of chopped prosciutto
½ pound of mozzarella cheese, grated
½ cup of grated Parmigiano Reggiano
Salt and pepper
Plus additional grated chesse for topping manicotti.

Mix together all of the ingredients for the filling and set aside.

To make the manicotti, cut the dough in half and roll halves on a well-floured pastry board into 2 thin sheets, no more than 1/16th of an inch thick. Cut into rectangles, 4 inches by 5 inches, and let dry for 1 hour. Cook rectangles for 10 to 12 minutes in rapidly boiling salted water. Drain and rinse with cold water and drain again. Spread a tablespoon or two of filling on each rectangle, roll, and close, pressing ends together to prevent the filling from leaking out. Place the manicotti, side by side, in a baking dish. Cover with Bolognese sauce and top with the grated Parmigiano Reggiano. Bake in hot oven (400 degrees) for 20 to 25 minutes. Serves 6 to 8 people.

Mamma's Manicotti

Before You Start,
"SLATE"

My dad gave me one year to make it in "the business," and then, if nothing panned out, I agreed to go to college and get a backup degree. So I took a chance and headed out alone, on my own, for the big city and Broadway (which was only a thirty-minute bus ride, since we lived in New Jersey), but that did sound good, didn't it? Who needed school? I knew how to act and sing. I had already done a musical. (You should read the reviews in my high school yearbook.) I knew I was going to make it. Who needed a backup plan? Unfortunately, when the year was up, I had no paying job; therefore, I had to live up to my part of the bargain. You see, even though I did get some theater work, I never got paying jobs—however, I did get an agent. Unfortunately, there was not a lot of work for a heavyset guy in my age group. I love that phrase, "heavyset guy." Right in that category is "stocky," or my favorite, "big boned." Come on. You know a fat person made those up. Big boned—I was fat, and that was starting to get in my way. More important, the year was going to be up on the coming Sunday. I only had a couple of days left to think of something. Knowing my dad, he was not going to wait a minute longer than necessary to talk to me about going to school.

My mom knew time was ticking away. She also knew I was panicking. She sat me down and suggested that maybe Dad was right and maybe I should go to school. I tried to convince her that I only needed a little more time and something was going to break. She smiled and said, "I'm not the one you need to convince. It's your dad." I stood up and told her I would tell him on Sunday—no ifs, ands, or buts. I thought I was so tough. My mom laughed and then told me she would help by using our secret weapon. That secret weapon was Mamma. See, whenever my mom or any of us had to give my dad bad news or needed something from him, we would have Mamma make his favorite meal—her famous stuffed eye round and her potato soufflé. The eye round was stuffed with prosciutto and seasonings and simmered in a deep pot with a large amount of delicious clear onion gravy. The potato pie was made with mashed potatoes and mozzarella, layered in a baking dish and baked. Does that not sound out of this world? Everyone really loved this dinner, especially Dad.

That Sunday when we sat down to dinner, Mamma brought out the roast, and my mom followed with the potato soufflé. It looked great. My dad's face lit up with anticipation for this mouthwatering dinner. Within seconds he knew something was up. His look of anticipation was replaced with a suspicious one. He looked at all of us and said, "All right, let me have it. What happened and who needs what?" Everyone looked at me. Before anyone could say a word, Mamma lifted the roast so my dad could smell it and suggested we eat first before everything got cold. One whiff and Dad was sold. I looked at Mamma, giving her a silent thank you. She bought me a little more time.

When dinner was over, I thought maybe I would get a break and my dad might have forgotten my year was up—but no such luck. He looked at me and said, "So—where do you want to go to college?" He said I could take some acting classes while working towards my bachelor of arts degree. I tried to explain to him that I did not want to go back to school. I knew how to act, and all I needed was a little more time. After we argued the subject for a while, my dad finally gave in—well, sort of. He told me that if I didn't go back to school, I would have to get a job, and I could pursue acting in my spare time. I agreed. I knew it wasn't going to be long before I got an acting gig, and I was right. Two days later I got my first commercial audition. My agent called and told me the audition would be sometime during the following week. Commercials paid very well. You received a paycheck every time it aired. These are called residuals. This was perfect! I could not wait to tell everyone. When I told Steven, he immediately asked: "Do you read a script or make lines up? Do they put you on tape? Do you wear costumes?" I told him I had no idea. Then he asked if the director would be there. He wanted to know how many people would be competing for the part. I started to get nervous. I had no idea what to expect.

When I arrived at the audition the following day, I took a deep breath and did what everyone else did. When they signed in, I signed in. They asked for the sides, I asked for mine, even though I had no idea what they were. When they handed them to me, I saw they were the part of the script I was going to read for the audition. When the others went over there lines, I did the same. While I was waiting to be called in, I overheard two of the actors taking about the school they were attending—the HB Studios. They were saying that it was expensive but so worthwhile. Man, I felt as if my dad had planted them there. Minutes later, I was called along with a ten-year-old boy who was going to read for the part of the little brother. The commercial was for an airline called Piedmont Airlines. It was about an older brother who was flying with his younger brother. As soon as I walked into the room, I spotted the director standing by the camera. I was extremely nervous, but I kept my cool. The director came over and gave us a few directions. Then he said, "Let's get it on tape." The camera was turned on, and the director turned to me and said, "Before you start, slate." I said, "Excuse me?" He again said, "Slate." I looked at him in confusion and said, "Slate?" He asked me again, this time annoyed, "Could you please slate?" Not knowing what to do, I put my two hands together pretending to make a clapboard. I clapped them together, smiled, and said, "Action." The director just looked at me in complete amazement. Then the ten-year-old standing next to me punched my arm and said, "It means say your name and your agent's name to the camera, you idiot." I wanted to die—hit the kid first, then die. To no one's surprise, I did not get the commercial.

It was a tough week. I had my first audition, and then my first realization that maybe I did need to go to class. I remembered the name HB Studios, the expensive school those two actors were discussing. That was the school I wanted to attend, but would my dad pay for just acting classes, not college? I would break the news to him this weekend. Hmm, what should Mamma make for Sunday dinner?

Mamma's Genoese Stuffed Eye Round

Ingredients:
12 ounces of coarsely chopped prosciutto (1-inch-thick slice)
3 tablespoon minced garlic
½ cup chopped parsley
1 cup grated Parmigiano Reggiano
½ cup olive oil
2- to 2½-pound eye round (have a butcher make a hole through the center of the eye round from one end to the other)
3 large onions, thinly sliced
3 (14-ounce) cans beef broth
4 cups water
Salt and pepper
Butcher's string

In a bowl, add 6 ounces of the chopped prosciutto, garlic, parsley, cheese, salt, pepper, and two tablespoons of oil. Mix together. Stuff the center of the roast one spoonful of stuffing at a time, using the end of a wooden spoon to push the stuffing all the way into the roast. Continue until the roast cannot take any more stuffing. Then tie the roast with butcher's string to keep stuffing in.

In a large pot, add the remaining oil and brown the roast, turning it to make sure all sides get browned. Add remaining prosciutto, sliced onions, broth, and water. Cover and simmer for 2 hours. Serves 6.

Mamma's Potato Soufflé

Ingredients:
5 pounds of potatoes, peeled and boiled
1½ sticks of butter
1 cup grated Parmigiano Reggiano
2 eggs
2 cups of heated milk
½ cup seasoned breadcrumbs
1 (16-ounce) package of mozzarella

Using a ricer, rice all the potatoes into a large bowl. (You can use a mixer if you prefer.) Add one stick of butter, Parmigiano Reggiano, and eggs. Mix while gradually adding the heated milk. Continue adding the milk until the mixture is stiff. Do not make as soft as regular mashed potatoes. They must be stiff. Using the remaining butter, grease a deep Pyrex dish or a pan. (Do not throw the butter away, as you will need what remains.) Coat the dish (or pan) with some of the breadcrumbs. Add a layer of the potato mixture and cover with slices of mozzarella. Add another layer of the potato mixture and another layer of mozzarella. Cover the top with the remaining potato mixture. Sprinkle with remaining breadcrumbs and dot with the remaining butter. Bake at 450 degrees for 20 minutes. Top should get browned. Serve immediately. Serves 8 to 10.

Greg's Reduced-Fat Potato Soufflé

Ingredients:
Substitute reduced-fat margarine for butter, 2% milk for regular milk, grated low-fat Parmigiano Reggiano for regular grated cheese and low-fat mozzarella for regular

Continue with same directions as original recipe.

Mamma's Genoese Stuffed Eye Round

Mamma's Potato Soufflé

They Don't Let Drag Queens on National TV

As you can see, Mamma did most of the cooking, especially Sunday dinner. My mom was very smart. When Mamma moved in with us, my mom realized that two women could not run a household, so mom went back to work, and Mamma ran the house. She cooked, did the laundry, cleaned the house, and took great care of us all. It's not as if we didn't want to help, but this was her thing, her job, and she took it very seriously. Mamma would get insulted if we all tried to do our own wash. We picked up after ourselves, but she dusted and vacuumed. I think having all these things to do in the home gave her a purpose and kept her young. That was my mom's plan—to make her feel needed and comfortable. As for the cooking, that was definitely Mamma's domain. No one cooked but Mamma, especially on Sundays; but that all changed the one Sunday when I cooked Sunday dinner.

Mamma was totally involved with a project for me, so I decided to give her a break and cook dinner. It all started with a TV show called Puttin' on the Hits for which I was dying to audition. See, my friend Steven (you know—Mr. VCR) and I always had a ball lip-syncing for each other. Sometimes we would lip-sync to a man's song and—oh, all right, we never did men. It's just that the women always had the best songs! When it came to lip-syncing, I would perform for anyone who was willing to watch. In my head, I was not a drag queen. After all, I never dressed in a costume or a wig or even used makeup—I was an actor. This was just another role to play. Steven, on the other hand, was a bank president. He only lip-synced for me.
I've known Steven my entire life. Not only was he my best friend, but also he was gay. I think that's the real reason why I was okay with myself at a young age. I mean, if one of the people you always looked up to was also gay, then how could it be wrong? My favorite number to perform was from Dreamgirls. You remember, the Broadway show with which I became obsessed. Well, that song, "And I'm Telling You I'm Not Going," I had down to a tee. I was Jennifer Holliday. Steven said I was better than any female impersonator he'd ever seen. I must tell you, I was good.

One evening, during dinner, I received a call from Steven. He could hardly talk. All he kept saying was, "Put on Channel 11! Put On Channel 11!" I ran to the TV and turned it on. Channel 11 showed a girl, dressed like Madonna, lip-syncing "Lucky Star." She sucked. Then I heard Steven yelling through the phone. "You have to do Jennifer! You have to do Jennifer!" I got back on the phone and asked him what the hell was I watching. He explained to me that this was a new show called "Puttin' on the Hits." I don't know if anyone remembers it. This show was in the '80s, and it was great. Each week people would lip-sync their favorite songs and costume themselves as the artists. I watched the rest of the show. One guy did, "Wake Me Up Before You Go Go," another girl imitated Cindy Lauper, and then a young man wowed everyone by lip-syncing, "Endless Love," with half of his face made up as Diana Ross and the other half as Lionel Richie. He was amazing. After the show, the credits listed a number to call for information on auditions.

The next day, Steven and I called and learned that there would be auditions at a mall in upstate New York, which was about an hour away. There was a catch. You had to mail in an application. Then they would randomly pick a hundred people to audition. Steven was sure I was going to get picked. I, on the other hand, refused to get excited about it until I heard from them. Deep down inside, I was excited. It's just that I was afraid to get my hopes up. I didn't even watch the show until I got another frantic call from Steven. I tuned in and saw a woman doing my song, "And I'm Telling You I'm Not Going." I sat there in shock. She sucked. Then, to make it even worse, the crowd loved it. To this day, I still think it was the song people loved, not her. Bitter? Table for one? I thought, "That's it. It's over." I felt they would never let someone repeat a song that had already been done on the show.

Of course, the way fate likes to screw around with me, the next day I got the letter that I had been picked to audition. Steven still thought I should just do the song, but I knew it would be a mistake. Then Steven suggested I do the other big song from the show, "I Am Changing." It was a great song, and Jennifer did it amazingly well; but it was not as well known as "And I'm Telling You I'm Not Going." Plus, what really made that number was the costume. When Jennifer started the song, she was in a skirt and a matching draped top. Towards the end of the song, the spotlight focused just on her head, leaving her body in darkness. On the words, "I am changing" Jennifer would undo the top of the dress and it would drop down, miraculously turning into a sequinned gown. When the spotlight opened up, Jennifer dramatically finished the song in the beautiful sequinned gown. To do this number, I needed the reversible dress. Where the hell would I get a dress like that? Just as if God was sending me the answer, Mamma walked in on cue.

I tried to explain how the dress worked—you know, the way it was a reversible dress. Mamma said she would think about it and see what she could do. For weeks she worked on the dress, I worked on the number, and Steven worked on the wig. Luckily, he had a friend who was a guy who had become a girl and was a hairdresser. Her name was Coco or Ralph, if you knew her years ago. He or she helped Steven, and the wig looked great. Sunday, the day before the audition, Mamma was still putting final touches on the dress. Thus, I decided to help by making Sunday dinner. I made Mamma's chicken cacciatora—pieces of chicken fried in oil, then cooked in a tomato sauce. This is a great dish. I have to tell you, when we sat down to dinner, everyone agreed it tasted terrific—not quite like Mamma's but pretty good for a first try. It was a little too salty, and I used a little too much oil; but I could see Mamma was impressed. Speaking of impressed, was I impressed when I saw the dress! It was flawless.

The poncho-type top (which was actually the red shiny dress turned inside out) and the skirt were blue. When you undid the Velcro, the top fell down creating a red shiny dress, which covered the blue skirt. Mamma did not use sequins, as they were much too expensive. When the transformation was done right on cue with the music, it was magical. Ralph, excuse me, I mean Coco, finished the wig and even lent me shoes. Where Coco got women's shoes in a size thirteen, I will never know. She also offered to do my makeup, which was great, because neither Steven nor I knew anything about makeup. Coco never called it "doing your makeup." She would say, "I am going to paint you, darling," and she did. She did it all, including false eyelashes, wax on my eyebrows, and women's eyebrows drawn over the wax. When she was done, I looked like a beautiful black woman.

Now let me tell you about the ride to the mall! I had no idea where Long Island was, but my brother had agreed to drive. All I told him was I had an audition, so off we went—Steven, my brother, my mom, and I. Sign-in was at 7:00 p.m. Everything was going great until we hit traffic. Steven was worried that we would not have time to finish getting ready, so he decided to start gluing my Lee Press-On Nails. There we were in my mom's station wagon—Steven trying to glue on those damn nails, which would go flying every time we hit a bump. You had to see the people's looks as we stopped at lights—me in drag and Steven trying to glue on my nails. I could see my brother looking at me through the rear view mirror. His face was expressionless, but I could see he was in shock. When we finally got there, we were really impressed.

The mall was closed to shopping and a big platform had been set up in the center. There must have been hundreds of people hanging out to watch the auditions. Suddenly, I started to think that maybe this was not such a good idea. Steven signed me in and gave them my music while I got dressed. When I was finally ready, I saw myself in the mirror. I looked good, if I had to say so myself. I looked as if I could have been in Dreamgirls. Then I heard the first person go on. I was ready. I felt like Norma Desmond getting ready for her close-up. Now all we had to do was wait until I got called.

As I looked around, I saw women dressed as Cher and Annie Lennox. One guy was doing Bruce, and there was a couple dressed up as John and Olivia from Grease; but I was the only guy dressed as a woman. What was even stranger, no one seemed to care. After two hours of waiting, I heard my number called. I took a deep breath, and as I walked on to the platform, I noticed the judges had this puzzled look on their faces. There was one exception—a very cute judge just had this big smile on his face. I smiled and started my number. Everyone loved it. Then came the big moment—I undid the top of the dress and right on cue, it fell into the gown. Everyone applauded. When I finished the song, I got a huge round of applause. Now don't ask me why, but as I was bowing, for some reason I decided to do my best Victor/Victoria. I stood up straight and very dramatically pulled off the wig. The crowd went crazy. The judges just sat there in shock. I realized that no one knew I was a guy except the one judge who had smiled at me when we came in. Also, by the look on their faces, they had no idea I was white. I bowed and walked off. I was a shoe-in. About an hour later, the judges got up, thanked everyone, and announced the people who would be appearing on the show. I listened but never heard my name. I didn't make it. At this point, my brother, who had not said a word the entire night, said there had to be a mistake. He told me I was the best thing up there. I just wanted to clean up and go home. As we were leaving, we saw one of the judges—the cute one who was smiling when I went on stage. He came over to me and told me he thought my number was fierce. That means "great" in gay talk. Yes, he was a sister. I asked him if I was that good, how come I didn't get on the show. He started to laugh. He said, "Did you really think they were going to let a drag queen on national TV? Oh, and not only a drag queen, but also a white guy doing a black woman?"

I was depressed for weeks. The only good thing that came from the whole experience was that Mamma began teaching me to make all her recipes and letting me cook dinner every once in a while. You know, it's funny. To this day, whenever I make Mamma's chicken cacciatora, I can't help remembering that first Sunday I made it for dinner and Mamma later teaching me how to make it correctly—and, of course, that fabulous reversible dress.

Mamma's Simple Chicken Cacciatora

Ingredients:
1 package whole chicken, cut up (cut each breast in half)
½ cup olive oil
½ cup white wine
2 cloves of chopped garlic
2 cans (28-ounce size) crushed tomatoes
Salt and pepper
½ cup chopped parsley

In a large pot, brown chicken in olive oil, a few pieces at a time. When finished browning, return all the chicken to the pot and add white wine. When the wine is dried up, remove the chicken and set aside. Remove some of the fat from the pan, if there appears to be too much left. Add garlic and sauté until brown. Add tomatoes and cook for about a half hour. Return chicken to the pot, add salt, pepper, and chopped parsley, and simmer until done, about 1 hour. Chicken should not be watery. Serves 6.

Mamma's Simple Reduced-Fat Chicken Cacciatora

Ingredients:
I package of whole chicken, cut up. (cut each breast in half)
½ cup white wine
2 tablespoons olive oil
2 cloves of chopped garlic
2 cans (28-ounce size) crushed tomatoes
½ cup chopped parsley
Salt and pepper

Bake chicken at 375 degrees for 10 minutes. Add wine and bake for additional 10 minutes. While chicken is baking, heat oil in a large pot. Sauté garlic in oil until brown, then add tomatoes, salt, pepper, and cook for 10 minutes. Add the chicken, the pan drippings, and the parsley to the tomatoes and simmer until done, about 1 hour. Chicken should not be watery. Seves 6.

Greg's Fat-Free Boneless Chicken Cacciatora

Ingredients:
Olive oil Pam spray
2 pounds boneless, skinless chicken breasts, cubed
½ cup white wine
2 cloves of chopped garlic
½ cup chopped parsley
2 cups sliced mushrooms
1 cup sliced green peppers
1 cup sliced red peppers
2 cans (28-ounce size) crushed tomatoes
Salt and pepper

Spray a large pot with Pam and sauté the chicken. As the chicken pieces begin to brown, gradually add the wine. Cook for 10 minutes. Add garlic, parsley, mushrooms, peppers, salt, and pepper. Stir and cook for 10 more minutes. Add the crushed tomatoes and cook for 40 minutes. Serve over brown pasta. Seves 6 to 8.

Mamma's Chicken Cacciatora

Reduced-Fat Chicken Cacciatora

"Time to Make the Donuts"

Well, Puttin' on the Hits was not going to make me a star—so for the next year all I did was take classes, audition during the day, and bartend at night. Fortunately, things were about to change with five simple words: "Time to make the donuts." I had gone on many auditions but just couldn't book anything. I tried to be everything they wanted, but it always seemed to be exactly what they didn't want. I could not do anything right, and most of the time, it wasn't even my fault. One time, I was auditioning for a commercial. I think it was for Starburst candy. All I knew about the commercial was what my agent had told me—they wanted people who looked like hippies. Naturally, I wore this great tie-dyed shirt and really cool specs. I looked—like an asshole. I was the only one dressed up. Then my manager sent me out for a commercial for Mead Notebooks—a "back to school" commercial. They were looking for heavyset guys who looked like wrestlers. The actors were going to wrestle for the Mead Notebook to show how durable it was. Actors my ass! When I walked into the room, it was filled with real wrestlers. The director wanted us to fake wrestle with each other. I had no idea what to do. It looked like I was trying to dance with the guy.

Acting class was not going very well either. I was used to just being myself—funny. But noooo—the teacher, who, I have to tell you, had no comic timing herself, never wanted me to be me. She said I always played for the joke. Duh, it's called "comedy." Between trying to make my teacher happy, trying to make my agent happy, and trying to be what the commercial people wanted, I was losing who I was. At this point, the only thing that was going right was my job at Bella Donna's. I worked for a great family—really nice people. The owner's wife was a character. Mitzi was her name. She was a cross between Norma Desmond and Cruella de Vil. When we got to work, she would be dressed in sweats, wearing no makeup, and vacuuming the restaurant. She would say a quick "hello," and then tell us what was happening for the night. Mitzi was all business. When she finished her chores, she would disappear upstairs (that's where they lived) not to return until the middle of the evening. When Mitzi came down to the restaurant, she would be dressed to the nines—from her pumps to her false eyelashes. Then she would get drunk and become the life of the party. She loved me; so when Mitzi partied, she let us all party. We would even sing with the pianist who worked there. That was a place where I could definitely be myself.

One afternoon I came home from a particularly bad audition. It was for a movie called Heaven Help Us. You remember that movie with a young Kevin Dillon. My agent had told me they liked me, but I had done everything they didn't want from the character. In nice terms, I sucked. I began to worry that if I didn't book something soon, my agent was going to drop me. I took a shower and went downstairs to get something to eat. Mamma was baking up a storm. Sunday was St. Joseph's Day, so she was making St. Joseph's zeppole. These zeppole are different from the ones you see at the Italian feasts. St. Joe's zeppole are fried rings of cream puff dough topped with custard cream and maraschino cherries. It sounds simple, but making zeppole is really a lot of work—but well worth it. Now that Mamma is gone, my mom and sister-in-law make them. It's a great once-a-year treat. Not only is it wonderful that this tradition is kept alive, but also it's something special that my mom and sister-in-law do together every year. That particular day, I sat down to watch Mamma in action. I loved watching her work. Since I still lived at home, we had these special times together quite often. I miss them. She noticed I was feeling down and asked how the audition went. I told her they didn't like me. She, being my Mamma, told me she could not understand how anyone could not like me. She said, "I'm sure everyone liked you. Are you being nice and respectful?" I laughed, "Yes, Mamma." Then she asked if I was being myself. I looked at her in confusion. She then said, "Don't let people intimidate you so you aren't yourself. Just be yourself, and people will love you." She gave me a kiss, and, even better, she gave me a spoonful of the cream she was making. I was eating the cream when it hit me. Was I being myself? That was it. I gave Mamma a big kiss. Like always, she knew how to save the day.

That week, things started to look up. I did my monologue in class, and for the first time, it worked. In fact, a girl in class, who was amazing herself, came up to me and told me how impressed she was with the monologue. Her name was Paula. You will hear more about her later. That same week I even got a great commercial audition for a new product called "New Coke," which never did take off. I was determined to book this commercial and was definitely prepared. I walked into the waiting room and looked at the other twenty people there. I gave them all my look of determination, which I had worked on all week. When I was called in to audition, I was ready. They told me to "slate," and I gave them my name and agent. I started doing the lines, being my bubbly self. They thanked me, and that was it. How could that be? I thought I was great. As I was grabbing my stuff, one of the casting people came out of the audition room. She told me the director was in the room during my audition. Even though he thought I was not right for this commercial, he loved me and wanted me to come back the next day to audition for a different commercial he was doing. I agreed, and before I could ask any questions, she was gone.

The next day I walked into the audition waiting room, ready to give the group my determined look; but I was taken back. There were only four actors waiting, and they all seemed to know one another. I felt myself slipping back to that previously nervous person. Then one of the four actors turned to me and asked if I was in the right place. He explained that this was the fourth callback for a national campaign for Dunkin Donuts. He continued to say that they were casting for the son of Fred, the donut maker. You know the guy—"Time to make the donuts!" My self-confidence was sinking fast. Right on cue, the same woman from the day before came in. She looked right at me and said, "Greg, you're here. Great! I'll tell the director." As she walked back to the audition room, the guy turned to me and said, "Guess you are in the right place. Funny, you don't look anything like Michael." I thought, "Who's Michael?" The women came back out and directed me to follow her. I took a deep breath and remembered what Mamma had said. When we were in the room, the director came over to introduce himself and Michael. "Oh, my God," I said. "You're the donut guy!" He laughed. The director explained that they were introducing the son of Fred. They told me the commercial was going to be about Fred's son waking up with his dad, getting dressed, and Dad teaching him the "family business." For the audition, all I had to do was say, in unison with Michael, "Time to make the donuts." To make a long story short, I booked it. I was myself and I booked it. That Sunday was the best St Joseph's Day ever. Not only was I eating Mamma's zeppole, but, thanks to her, I was eating them as a working, paid actor.

Mamma's St Joseph's Zeppole

Ingredients:
1 cup hot water
½ cup butter
¼ teaspoon salt
1 cup all-purpose flour
3 large eggs or 4 small ones
Parchment paper
Frying oil (I use Crisco oil)

In a 2-quart saucepan, combine the water, butter, and salt. Place the mixture over medium heat and bring to a simmer, stirring a few times. As soon as the butter is melted, bring quickly to a boil and add the flour all at one time, stirring briskly and constantly until it begins to leave the sides of the pan (it will look like dough). Remove from the heat at once and stir until smooth and velvety. Set aside to cool. (This is important because adding eggs to a hot mixture will partially cook them, and they will lose much of their leavening properties.)

When mixture has cooled, add the eggs one at a time, beating vigorously after each addition. You may use an electric mixer or an electric hand mixer for this, as mixing by hand would be difficult and require considerable strength. When all the eggs have been added, the mixture should be smooth and thick. (You may prepare and refrigerate this mixture ahead of time. Bring to room temperature when you are ready to fry the zeppole.)

Cut the parchment paper into 24 (4½- to 5-inch) squares. Fill a pastry bag fitted with a ½-inch star tip with the dough. Squeeze out on the pieces of parchment paper a circle of dough, making a ring about 3½ inches in diameter. In a 10- or 12-inch skillet, heat 2 inches of oil to 375 to 380 degrees and fry the zeppole, a few at a time. Place the zeppole in the oil with the parchment paper. As the zeppole starts to brown, it will slip off the parchment. Using tongs, remove the parchment paper after about 10 seconds.

The zeppole should be fried slowly to a medium golden color, turning once when the first side has reached the desired color. Drain the zeppole on paper toweling or other absorbent paper. When well drained, they should be stored at room temperature on a flat surface. Do not place them on top of one another. The zeppole should be fried as close to the serving time as possible, no more than the day before. Yields 11 to 12.

Mamma's Pastry Cream

Ingredients:
1 quart of milk
1 cup of sugar
1 cup of all-purpose flour
4 eggs
4 teaspoons of vanilla

Put all of the above ingredients in a blender and mix for a few seconds until well blended. Put the mixture in the top half of a double boiler. Cook over hot (not boiling) water, stirring constantly, until the mixture is thick. This should take about 20 or 30 minutes. Cool cream. Stir in vanilla, then refrigerate until ready to use.

Note: When cooling the cream, put a piece of wax paper over the top half of the double boiler and cover. The wax paper will prevent a crust from forming on the surface of the cream.

When ready to serve, place a teaspoonful of the custard cream on top of the zeppole on two sides. On each mound of cream place a half or a quarter of a maraschino cherry.

Mamma's St Joseph's Zeppole

I Put a Spell on You

By now, I'm sure you're all getting to the point where you're thinking, "Oh, come on, no one's life is that great. Where's the pain, the suffering, the fighting? What were they, the friggin' Waltons?" I have to tell you, we kind of were. I mean, we did fight, and we did have problems (remember me and food), but it was nothing out of the ordinary. No one drank too much or had a drug problem. No one beat anyone or had any deep, dark secrets. Actually, we were very boring. We were a family who really liked being with each other. Of course, this does not mean I had a perfect life. As for the commercial, it had been six months, and the jobs were not coming in as fast as I thought they would. I quit Bella Donna's and I could not get an audition. Yes, I had a perfect family, but not a perfect life. Also, have you noticed that in all my chapters I have never brought up a boyfriend, a lover, or a significant other? That's because when it came to relationships, I had no luck. In fact, you can say I had bad luck. Actually, let's just say it sucked—and still does. At forty-something, I am still alone—great family, great friends, but no special someone, no soul mate—but I'm hopeful. I still feel like Snow White—some day my prince will come. Actually, at this point a duke would do! Who am I kidding? One of the Seven Dwarfs would look good to me. The problem is I always seemed to fall in love with the wrong guy. In addition, when I fell, I fell hard. I am a hopeless romantic. I have always wanted what I saw in the movies—soundtrack and all. You know what I'm talking about. I would be somewhere, and all of a sudden I would turn around and see him. He would see me. Our eyes would lock, and then, out of nowhere, we would hear Endless Love. As my friends would often remind me, "That only happens in the movies." I always felt that it would be great if we could pick a movie or sitcom in which to live. Think about it. How cool would that be? Back to reality—all the guys I have dated sucked. The weird thing is that Mamma could always recognize the "bad" ones, which, in my case, were usually all of them. I would bring someone home to meet the family, and immediately she would know if he was nice or an asshole. Let me see, she didn't like Tony. He ended up being a compulsive liar. Chris—Mamma said he was hiding something. Maybe the fact that he slept with anything with a pulse? Chuck—he was nasty—hated everyone and everything. Al was always confused—Monday gay, Tuesday straight. You get the point. Can I pick them or what? Then there was Glen. Glen and I worked at a hotel. When my commercial stopped airing, I needed to make money. I needed a job, and I was too embarrassed to go back to Bella Donna's. After all, I was supposed to be a star by then. Glen worked in the kitchen, and I bartended. Now, you have to understand, Glen was straight, nineteen, and hot. At work, he never spoke to me except to ask for a soda.

From this point on, you will probably think I'm making this up; but it's the absolute truth. I went to Boston to visit a friend for the weekend. On Saturday, we decided to go to Salem. I stopped in a witch's store to browse, and I spotted prepackaged spells. I found one that promised to "bring you true love." The directions stated that you had to leap through a field, naked, at midnight, throwing special petals around while chanting three times, "Come to me, true love. I am waiting and willing. Come to me, true love. Come to me, please." Who would spend money on this? I would. The following week I tried the spell.

When everyone was asleep, there I was in my backyard (it was a very large backyard) about to step out of my robe and leap about naked. Thanks to a joint I had smoked in my room, I was good to go. Yes, there I was, naked, in the backyard, leaping and throwing my petals, saying the "magic words." I was so proud, until I turned around and saw my grandmother looking through the kitchen window. She smiled, waved, and walked away. We never spoke of it.
The next day Glen asked for his usual soda, but this time he started up a conversation. The next thing you know, we hung out a couple of times, and within a few weeks, we started to date. He explained to me that he had never dated a guy before. His exact words: "I'm not into guys. I'm just into you." Who was I to argue? He was nineteen, and I was twenty-four. Need I say more? We had such a great time together. He was a jock and an outdoor type of guy. He wanted to share his love of the outdoors with me and started by introducing me to fishing. In fact, one weekend we went fishing in Lake George, where I caught my first fish. Now get this—he actually made me gut and clean it. I felt so "macho."

The next weekend was my time to share, and I took him to see Les Miserables on Broadway. He fell in love with the show. The next day he went out and bought the CD, which he played every day. That Christmas I made him a collage of different scenes from the show, which I put under glass and framed. He loved it. We really had a blast together. I took him to see Gypsy with Tyne Daly, and he taught me how to shoot pool. I introduced him to the museums, and he introduced me to hiking. I opened a new world for him, and he did the same for me. The day I brought him home to meet Mamma (by now I knew enough to bring any new guy to meet Mamma before I fell for him), she was making her chocolate ricotta pie. This is a special pie she made only for Easter. I introduced Mamma to Glen, and they hit it off immediately. I guess that was because he wanted to be a chef and was going to the Culinary Institute of New York the following year. He recognized Mamma's talent and was interested in watching her prepare the pie. After a few minutes, he started asking Mamma questions, and before I knew it, Mamma was showing him how to make the dough for the chocolate ricotta pie. They were so cute together. My grandmother liked him. Thank God, because I did, too.

Glen and I had a blast for about a year, but when he went to school, things changed. He was nineteen and wanted to go to parties and to meet new people. In fact, he met one very special person, Lorrie. He didn't hide this from me. In fact, he felt that it was not cheating since he was with a girl. Right then I knew this was no longer going to work. There was a whole world he needed to experience, and he was not going to come home every weekend to see me. As hard as it was for me, I ended it. I told him that if it was meant to be, we would be together again. He was pissed and felt that I was abandoning him, but I knew it was the best thing for the both of us. I did not hear from him again. Six months later, his friend Paul contacted me. Paul was the only person in Glen's life who knew about us. Paul told me that Glen had died in a car accident. I was heartbroken, but I kept it together. Steven came with me to the wake because I was very nervous. I did not want to lose it in front of Glen's family, as no one knew about our relationship. Steven walked in first, and quickly turned to me, telling me to take a deep breath. Then I saw why. On one side of the casket, there were pictures of Glen's family and friends. On the other side of the casket, his family had displayed my Les Miserables collage on an easel. I knew right then how much Glen had cared for me. His mom came over to me and took my hand. She told me how much that collage meant to Glen. Then she smiled and told me how much I meant to Glen. Did she know? I have no idea. All I knew was I had been very blessed to have had him in my life. Even if it was for a short time, I was still blessed. You know, sometimes when I'm cooking, I think about when those two special people in my life shared the day making the Easter ricotta pies, laughing together and giving me one amazing memory that often gets me through the day.

Mamma's Chocolate Ricotta Pie

This recipe is for 2 pies

Crust

Ingredients:
½ pound of butter or margarine
¾ cup of sugar
3 eggs
4 cups of all-purpose flour

Cream butter or margarine, add sugar, and cream again. Add eggs and mix well. Mix in flour to form dough. Wrap in wax paper sprinkled with flour and place in refrigerator until ready to use. It should be at room temperature when used.

Filling

Ingredients:
8 eggs, separated
1 pound of sugar
1 tablespoon of vanilla
Grated orange and lemon rind, if desired
3 pounds of ricotta
2 cups chocolate bits

Beat yolks, add sugar, and beat until lemon colored. Add vanilla and granted orange and lemon rind. Add ricotta and mix until creamy. Add chocolate bits and stir slightly to mix in bits. Beat egg whites until stiff and fold into mixture. Pour into unbaked shells. Use 10-inch Pyrex dishes. Bake in 350-degree oven until golden—about 1 to 1½ hours.

Note: After 1 hour, check pie. If it looks golden, use a cake tester to test the filling. If the tester comes out clean, the pie is done. If some filling sticks to the tester, check the pie every ten minutes until tester comes out clean.

Mamma's Chocolate Ricotta Pie

A Night of Illusion

Well, the next couple of years were not the greatest. I was working through the loss of Glen. My career was going nowhere. I was back working at Bella Donna's, as I could not bear to stay at the hotel where Glen and I had worked. I was gaining my weight back, and, yes, I was still living at home. I was such a joy to be around! At this point, I wondered if I really wanted to do the acting thing. I was almost twenty-seven. I decided, for the time being, I would just wait tables, make money, and try to find something else to do with my life.

At home, everything was the same. Mom and Mamma were still doing Sunday dinner. We were now twelve, which included spouses, two nieces, and two more nephews. I could tell my dad was getting nervous about what I was going to do with my life. He never discouraged me, but I could tell he was worried. Not to fear—a new business venture was just around the corner.

It all started one night after work when we were all hanging out at the restaurant after hours for a meeting. A meeting meant that Mitzi (remember the cross between Norma Desmond and Cruella de Vil) was bored and wanted company. No one minded, because she let us drink the entire evening. My friend Lisa (also an aspiring actress) and I got a big kick spending time with Mitzi. One night, while we were hanging out, Mitzi told us that we needed to do something to pick up business. I thought, "We? This was not my restaurant." Then she asked me if I could maybe direct a show—a musical like "South Pacific." A dinner show is what she had in mind. I explained to her it would cost too much. She would need to hire musicians and rent costumes—not to mention there wasn't enough room in the restaurant. Once she heard what it would cost, she dropped the idea.

A couple of days later, Steven and I were hanging out at my house. My mom and Mamma were in the kitchen making cookies—Mamma's famous pignoli cookies. Mamma called us in to taste a few that had just cooled off, so Steven, my mom, Mamma, and I sat around the table having a cozy coffee klatch. For some reason, my work came up in the conversation. Everyone could tell something was wrong by the look on my face. I told them that I was worried—if business at the restaurant didn't pick up soon, I would be out of a job. Steven told me not to worry, as something would come up. Then he handed me a cookie, saying, "For now just enjoy." He smiled at Mamma and said, "These are like a taste of heaven. I'd do anything for these cookies." He was right. I took one bite, and "wham," I felt better. I laughingly told them how Mitzi asked me to put on a show to attract more customers, but I explained that a show would be far too expensive. Mamma, who was always supportive, said, "Why not do what you did at your party? Have your friends dress up as their favorite character and pretend to sing? That won't cost much, will it?" We all started to laugh. I said, "Oh yeah, people are going to pay to see me and my friends in a dress." Steven, who at that point was laughing so hard he was almost choking, answered, "Yeah, like one of those drag shows from the club!" I stopped laughing. Then

Steven stopped laughing and looked at me. He said, "You know, you could do it." I thought to myself, "I really could."

That night I called Lisa and pitched the idea to her. Once she was on board, we both pitched it to Mitzi the next day at work. She loved the idea of putting on a La Cage show. Each performer took care of his own music, makeup, and costumes. No cost to her—why wouldn't she love it? She had a sound system, and I knew someone who could do the lighting. All Lisa and I wanted was 30% of each ticket sold. She agreed. Now came the big question: how do you find the performers here in West Caldwell, N.J.? Well, if you don't know any better, you put an ad in the local paper. Wait, it gets better. Then, you have the auditions in a church basement. What were we thinking? The ad read: "Wanted for a show. Female impersonators who do celebrities." I included the time, date, etc. I also contacted Coco. You remember Coco—he or she, take your pick. I asked if she would invite her friends to audition, and she agreed. This was great—everything was working out perfectly, so I thought.

The night of the auditions, I showed up carrying a box of small bags filled with homemade cookies. Mamma felt that if we did not hire certain people, maybe it would soften the blow if we handed them a pouch of homemade cookies. Don't laugh. If I had been given a bag of cookies after bombing at an audition, I would definitely have felt better. Lisa and I sat at a long table, waiting for the candidates, but something was wrong. The first guy came in and did Donald Duck and then Popeye. The second person came in and told us he was doing Sean Connery, and then stood before us and said, "Bond. James Bond." We had another guy who stood there and yelled, "Stella, Stella." At this point, I got so nervous, I began stuffing cookies down my throat to stop laughing. Then it happened. A man walked in who looked just like Ann-Margret—wig, tights, and all! I was so happy. I thought to myself, "This must be a friend of Coco's." He introduced himself and asked if there was a place for him to change. "He wants to change," I thought. He was already in complete drag, but then, one never knows. This guy could be psychotic—so I pointed him to the bathroom. When he came back, he was wearing a long red dress. He did a Vegas number that I had never heard before. When he was finished, I asked him if he could do "Bye Bye Birdie." That was an Ann-Margret number that everyone knew. He answered, "Ann doesn't do 'Bye Bye Birdie' anymore." I responded by saying, "I'm not asking Ann—I'm asking you." As he started to gather his stuff, he noticed that there was no one else around. He asked if I was having a problem finding the right people. I laughed and told him we did have some unexpected characters auditioning. He said he thought he knew why. He showed me the ad in the paper. No wonder—the paper had edited my ad. They eliminated the word "female." It read that we were looking for "celebrity impersonators."

After a while, some of Coco's friends came in. One did Judy. Then there was a Diana Ross and a great Wynonna Judd. Things were looking up; and by the end of the night, we had three people sent by Coco and a Donald Duck. He actually was a good comedian, so I used him as the host. Last but not least, we had Ann-Margret, the psycho. Lisa was worried that there were not enough acts, even if each person did two numbers. She was ready to give up, but I still had some tricks up my sleeve. After the auditions, I went over to Steven's apartment. I told him about all the people I had hired and surprised him with the news that I had decided to be in the show myself. I was going to perform my Jennifer number and put together an Ethel Merman song. I continued to tell him that we had no Cher; and while all these guys were very good, they did not come close to his performance at my party. That said, I took out a bag of Mamma's pignoli cookies and offered one to Steven. He took one look at the cookies and stopped me right then and there, saying there was no way he was doing this show—cookies or not. He proceeded to tell me that a party was one thing, but no way was he doing his act for strangers. He was concerned that one of his customers from the bank might see him. I said, "What a shame. No one does medleys like you do." Even though he was vehemently refusing to perform, he had pulled out his Cher wig and had started to comb it out. I kept telling him how much I needed him. While he was combing out the wig, he said to me, "If I do the show, and I do mean 'if,' I would start with 'old Cher' and finish the performance with 'new Cher.'" I told him that was a great idea. He continued to tell me that "if" he did it, he would have to have a stage name, so no one would know who he was. By the end of the night, all the cookies were gone; and not only did he have his whole number planned from the music to the costume, but also "Pepper Saint Clair" was born.

Once rehearsals started, I worked everyone hard. I put together great opening and closing numbers. The actors chose their own characters, songs, and costumes. Everything moved along extremely well. In fact, everybody agreed it was their best experiences doing shows. The show was a huge hit, and everyone did a terrific job. Steven's Cher number outdid his performance at my party. We sold out all three shows that weekend. After the last show, all the performers came to me in the dressing room, wanting to know where the next gig was. When were we performing again? I hadn't even considered that. Could we book the show in other places?

My mom and Mamma came into the dressing room and gave me a big hug. They told me how proud they were of me. I told them the other performers thought I should book the show in other places. They both thought that was a great idea. Then, out of the corner of my eye, I saw Steven taking off his makeup. I wondered how I was going to get him to do more shows. Then it hit me. I turned to Mamma and said, "I think you'll need to make more cookies."

Mamma's Pignoli Cookies
(Cookies are cookies. Just enjoy.)

Preheat oven to 350 degrees.

Ingredients:
1½ pounds almond paste
1½ cups sugar
1 cup confectioners' (powdered) sugar
4 egg whites
2 cups pignoli nuts (pine nuts)
Parchment Paper

Break up almond paste into pebblelike pieces. Combine almond paste with sugar, confectioners' sugar, and egg whites. Use an electric mixer and mix ingredients on low speed until blended. Increase speed to medium and continue mixing for an additional 2 minutes. The dough will be sticky, so keep a bowl of water nearby to wet your fingers before rolling each cookie to keep the dough from sticking to your fingers. Roll dough into 1-inch balls and then roll balls in pine nuts. Place cookies 2 inches apart on cookie sheet lined with parchment paper. Lightly flatten cookie with spoon. Bake 15 to 20 minutes. Allow to cool completely before removing from parchment with a metal spatula.

Makes 50 cookies

Mamma's Pignoli Cookies

If the Girdle Fits...

Yes, the show was a big success. As a result, Lisa and I started booking the show in a variety of places. We were hired for fundraisers, comedy clubs, and dinner theaters. As a matter of fact, I incorporated a few additional characters in my repertoire. The problem was that not only were the shows getting bigger, but so was I. One night, when I went to put on my Ethel Merman dress, I was not able to zip it up, and this was not the first time that happened. Mamma had already let it out twice. Thank God one of the performers had a cape, which was part of his Wonder Woman costume for the song "I Need a Hero." There I was, on stage, lip-syncing an Ethel Merman number with a red, white, and blue cape over me. I looked like an old, fat, deranged superhero. It was not a pretty sight. When I got home, I put on the dress to show Mamma, and she sadly told me there was no material left to let out. I thought I was screwed until I remembered that all the real drag queens from the show wore full-piece girdles. Maybe that would work, but where would I find one? Where else? Macy's!!

The next day Mamma and I went on our journey for the girdle. I was so nervous, but not Mamma. She went right into the store and asked the sales woman if she had XXL woman's under garments. The sales woman smiled and said, "I think you would need a medium." Mamma, without missing a beat, said, "Oh, it's not for me. It's for my grandson." I just stood there, smiling; but deep inside me I wanted to die—but not because of what you're thinking. I did not care that we were shopping for a girdle. I was actor, and it was part of a costume. It was because I needed a size XXL. The sales woman looked me over in judgment and then pointed to the back of the store. After a few minutes of Mamma taking different garments out of the boxes and holding them against me, she finally found one she thought would fit. I thought the torture was over, but Mamma said, "Now go try it on." I loved Mamma, but at that point I thought she had lost her mind. I went into the men's dressing room, waited a few minutes, and then came out and told her it fit perfectly. Thank God when I got home and tried it on, it did fit.

That night I was in my room working on some new characters for the show when I caught a glimpse of myself in the mirror. I was shocked at what I saw. I had not realized how much weight I had gained. It forced me to think about my weight problem—about how much weight I had gained over the years, not to mention all the diets that I had tried. Why could I not keep the weight off once I lost it? I was like a yoyo—up the scale and down the scale over and over again. It's not as if I had never tried to diet. My God! I must have tried every diet in the book. I counted points, had prepackaged food delivered to my home, drank shakes instead of meals, ate only low-fat foods, eliminated carbs, etc., etc. You name it, and I tried it. I even went to a diet doctor in New York City, Dr. Stuart Berger, who wrote, The Immune Power Diet.

My poor mother and I went on this venture together, and it proved to be the hardest diet ever! The diet was based on the premise that the body was allergic to certain foods, and those allergies prevented one from losing weight. Based on the results of blood work, Dr. Berger would eliminate these foods from your diet—foods that included wheat, dairy, rice, certain meats and vegetables, sugar—any food sensitivity that showed up in your blood work. As a result, we ate nothing but lean protein and steamed vegetables for a total of 800 calories a day. Also, we could only have natural foods, so also eliminated were artificial sweeteners. No caffeinated beverages were allowed. That meant no coffee for mom and no Tab for me. The first week of the diet was unbearable and depressing. I was so depressed that I went to complain to my mother. I went to her room, and she was lying on the bed in tears. Poor thing was having withdrawals from caffeine. This was a woman who drank espresso for breakfast. The diet proved to be successful, and we did lose weight. I lost over a hundred pounds, and my mother got down to a size 8. We thought the doctor was a genius. On 800 calories a day, what else? Unfortunately, when I went off the diet, I gained back a lot of the weight—so did my mom.

Anyway, my mirror reflection depressed me, and I remained depressed for several days. I had to force myself to snap out of it, at which time I made the resolution to get back on the diet trail. I decided to try that famous Florida diet—you could eat as much as you wanted, but only the prescribed foods. I showed Mamma what I was allowed to eat, and she agreed to cook my meals accordingly. That night Mamma made her incredible beef stew for dinner. It was made with tender beef cubes, peas, carrots, onions, and potatoes, all smothered in a wonderful brown sauce—but not for me. Instead, she made me a simple veal stew, which was served with fresh tomatoes and a medley of low-calorie vegetables. It may have been made dietetically, but, I have to tell you, it was great. It was so delicious that I had two big dishfuls. I remember Mamma saying, "I know that it's dietetic, but I don't know how you can lose weight eating that much." I thought about it, and maybe she was right. I looked at her plate. While mine was filled to the brim, her portion was just large enough to fit on the plate, with a little room to spare. Of course, I dismissed the thought and went on following the diet the way I considered to be correct. I stayed on the diet for six months. All I ate was the diet dinners that Mamma prepared for me. All right, that's not all I ate. Remember what I said in the first chapter? Some receipts you can't change, and you should enjoy them as life's little pleasures. Well, I sneaked in a few "little pleasures" once in a while, but I did lose weight, and I'm proud to say that "Ethel" did not need to wear a girdle after that. The question was: would Greg?

Mamma's Beef Stew

Ingredients:
½ cup olive oil
3½ pounds of boneless sirloin steak, cut into 1-inch cubes (you may also use beef chuck already cut in cubes)
2 cloves of minced garlic
2 onions, sliced ½-inch thick
2 cups of beef broth
1 cup red wine
5 carrots, cut into 1-inch pieces
5 stalks of celery, cut into 1-inch pieces
2 cups of crushed tomatoes
2 cups frozen peas
3 tablespoons ketchup
2 tablespoons Worcestershire sauce
2 bay leaves
½ cup chopped parsley
3 potatoes, cut into large chunks
Salt and pepper to taste

In a large pot, heat oil and brown meat for about 10 minutes. Add garlic and onions and sauté for another 5 minutes. Season with salt and pepper. Add beef broth and wine and bring to a boil. Lower heat and add the carrots, celery, crushed tomato, peas, ketchup, Worcestershire sauce, bay leaves and parsley. Simmer on a low heat for 45 minutes. Add potatoes and simmer for another 45 minutes. Add water if needed. Serves 6 to 8.

Greg's Healthy Reduced-Fat Veal Stew
Ingredients:
Substitute veal for beef, sweet potatoes instead of white potatoes, olive oil Pam for olive oil, and add 2 cups of any broth.

Spray a large pot with Pam and brown veal for about 10 minutes, gradually adding 1 cup of broth so it does not burn. Continue directions from above. Serves 6 to 8.

Mamma's Beef Stew

Greg's Healthy Reduced-Fat Veal Stew

Ingredients:

Substitute veal for beef, sweet potatoes instead of white potatoes, olive oil Pam for olive oil, and add 2 cups of any broth.

Spray a large pot with Pam and brown veal for about 10 minutes, gradually adding 1 cup of broth so it does not burn. Continue directions from above. Serves 6 to 8.

Greg's Reduced-fat Veal Stew

Eventually, We All Slow Down

The show ran for about two years, but eventually the number of bookings started to dwindle. It had run its course; and to tell you the truth, I was starting to get bored. Even Steven stopped performing. I decided that after this last big show, I was going to bow out and the performers could book the shows themselves. I also had gained the weight back that I had lost last year on the famous Florida diet. Why? Because I still had not learned the secret—portion control. That meant that Mamma was gradually letting the dress out again, but she never minded.

I remember one particular time when Mamma was fitting me for one of the costumes. She was getting very frustrated because the hem was not hanging evenly. This was unusual for her, and it made me realize that she was starting to slow down—not much, but she was in her late '80s. Mamma wasn't moving as fast as she did in the past, and trust me, that fact did not sit well with her. It was so cute how she used to test herself to make sure she wasn't slowing down. I discovered her little trick one day when I was watching her make homemade cappelletti (little hats). These are similar to the tortellini you put in soup. I can still see her in her red apron, working at the table. Now this is what impressed me: in order not to slow down, she would time herself to see how long it would take to make the first 100 cappelletti. Then she would make sure it would take the same amount of time or less to make each additional 100. That day she was getting very frustrated, because she was taking more time then she had allowed herself. Mamma was being very hard on herself. I was taken back by this fact, because Mamma rarely screwed up, but when she did, we would just laugh about it, because it was never a big deal.

I remember one particular mistake over which we had a huge laugh. It was the first time she made jambalaya. I was just a kid, and I was hanging out watching her cook—something I did often at that time. Everything was going great, and she was a very pleased with herself. When it was all done, she gave me a small bowl to taste. I took a big mouthful, and within seconds my eyes began to water. I felt as if someone was stealing my saliva. My lips started to burn, and then my whole mouth was on fire. I jumped up, ran to the sink, and drank the water right out of the faucet. When I caught my breath, I turned around and there was my Mamma. She smiled and said, "Too much cayenne powder?" "You think?" I asked. Then we both had a good laugh—as I said, no big deal.

Then there was the time when cousins from Italy were coming to stay with us for a while. Cousin Paulo's favorite dish was Mamma's escargot in red gravy (I know—tomato sauce to some of you, but let me tell you, the escargot in red gravy are far better than the usual butter sauce). Escargot must be kept alive until cooking time, just like mussels and lobster. Mamma kept the snails in a big pot of water with a screen over it, so they could breathe but not escape. They intrigued me, so before we left to pick up the cousins at the airport, I had to hold one, of course. I even named him, Ralph. When we got back, were we in for a surprise! I had left the cover off, and the snails were crawling up the walls and across the ceiling. I thought everyone was going to kill me, especially Mamma. She had warned me not to touch the screen cover. At first I thought she was going to lace into me, but after the initial shock, she just gave me that special smile and laughed it off. This was my screwup, but she took it in her stride. She calmly instructed us to catch the snails. What a sight—all of us standing on chairs trying to gather up all the snails. We succeeded, and that night we had escargot for dinner, and they were delicious!

Another time comes to mind, when she was making me a costume for the high school production of Damn Yankees. She had made me a mambo costume for my number. Mamma worked on it for weeks. A couple of days before the show, I had my last fitting. When I tried it on, the sleeves were too short. (Remember, Mamma made all my costumes without a pattern.) I thought she was going to lose it. Instead, she calmly told me to stick around, because she had to redo the sleeves. Then she took the scissors and just tore into the sleeves. Don't ask me how, but she fixed them. Maybe she did lose her cool sometimes, but we never saw it. The day she got so mad and frustrated about how long it was taking her to make the cappelletti, I realized for the first time that Mamma was getting old and was not going to be here forever. I sat down with her and tried to help. We hung out that entire afternoon. After she relaxed a bit, she resumed her original pace. I was very happy that I spent that day with her, talking and laughing. She told me many stories about her youth, her hopes, and her dreams. It was a day I will never forget, as I learned so much about the person, not just the grandmother. Oh, and of course, when we were done, I got a small bowl to taste.

Homemade Chicken Soup

Ingredients:
1 whole soup chicken (a hen makes a tastier soup, but you may use a roaster)
6 carrots, halved
6 stalks of celery, halved
1 large onion
1 (28-ounce) can plump whole tomatoes with juice
4 to 6 bouillon cubes
Salt to taste

Put the chicken, carrots, celery, onion, salt, and tomatoes in a large soup pot and cover with cold water. Simmer over medium heat for 1 hour. Add the bouillon and simmer for ½ hour more or until chicken falls off bone. Take everything out of the pot and put aside. Pour soup through strainer to remove any pieces that you might have missed. Let soup cool and then refrigerate to allow all the fat to come to the top. Skim before using. Note: If you are using the broth for the cappellettis, then you can use the chicken and vegetables for another dinner. Just cut up chicken and vegetables, add some pasta, and you have chicken vegetable soup.

Mamma's Cappelletti (or Tortellini) for Soup

Ingredients:
½ pound loin of pork
2 boneless chicken breasts
2 tablespoons butter
4 ounces of Marsala
¼ pound boiled ham (or prosciutto if you are not freezing them)
¼ pound mortadella
Salt and pepper
½ cup grated Parmigiano Reggiano
Nutmeg to taste
One whole egg and one egg yolk (save egg white to seal the cappelletti)

Cut pork and chicken breasts into small pieces. Melt butter in a frying pan and sauté meat over high heat, stirring constantly. When the meat is partly cooked, add the Marsala, a little at a time, while continuing to stir. When the liquid has dried, remove the frying pan from the heat and add the ham (or prosciutto) and the mortadella. Put this mixture through a food grinder to obtain a fine, smooth, pastelike mixture. Add salt and pepper, the grated Parmigiano Reggiano, the nutmeg, the whole egg and the yolk, mixing everything until well blended.

Note: If you prefer not to make Mamma's homemade dough below, you may use premade wonton sheets that may be purchased from most supermarkets. If you choose to use wontons then continue instructions at the asterisk below.

Dough for Cappelletti

Ingredients:
4 cups all-purpose flour (1 pound), plus extra to flour hands and board
½ teaspoon salt
3 eggs
Water to make a medium to stiff dough

Makes about 320 cappelletti

Sift flour with salt onto a large pastry board to form a well, leaving some flour at the bottom of the well. Break eggs into the center of the well and scramble with a fork. With your hands, gradually pull flour in from the sides. Keep pushing up the flour on the outer wall of the well to keep the sides from breaking. The eggs will absorb the flour, forming sticky dough. At this time, begin to add the water slowly, a little at a time, to form a medium to stiff dough, adding more flour if necessary. Sprinkle the board with flour and knead 10 minutes. Don't let the dough get dry. If it starts to appear too dry, slowly add drops of water to soften. The dough should be elastic but not sticky. As you knead, the dough will stick to your hands. Scrape your fingers and dust with a little flour before you start kneading again. Cover the dough and let it stand for 2 hours.

Cut the dough in half or in quarters and roll out one half or one quarter at a time. Cover the rest of the dough with wax paper and place in a bowl to keep from drying out. Roll dough out very thin on a well-floured pastry board. Dough should not be more than 1/16th of an inch thick.
* Using a round cookie cutter 1½ inch in diameter cut rolled dough into circles. Put 1 teaspoon

of the filling in center of each circle. Brush the edge of the circle with the egg white and fold over the dough, pressing edges to seal, thus forming a semicircle. Bring ends of semicircle together, twisting and pressing together in a ring effect, forming a little hat. Arrange cappelletti separately on a floured tablecloth to dry. These can be prepared a few days ahead and refrigerated until ready to use, or they can be frozen for several weeks.

Note: Drop the cappelletti (fresh or frozen) in boiling chicken broth and cook for about 15 minutes. Serve with grated Parmigiano Reggiano cheese.

Note: Capelletti may also be served with tomato sauce. Drop them in boiling, salted water, and cook for about 20 minutes. Drain and serve with Bolognese sauce (or your favorite sauce) and grated Parmigiano Reggiano cheese.

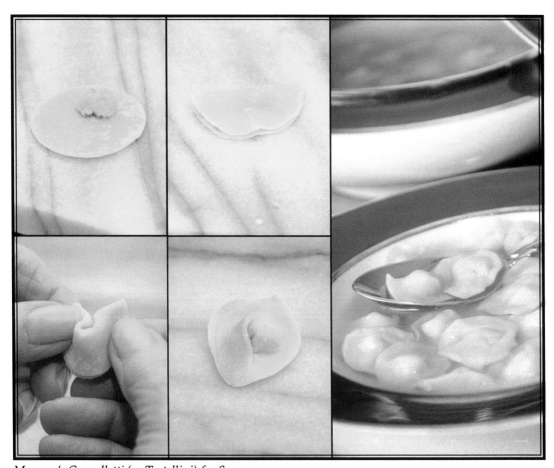

Mamma's Cappelletti (or Tortellini) for Soup

"You're a Little Heavy and You're Leaning on Me"

It was autumn—my favorite time of the year. It always reminded me of Glen, because he loved the outdoors. I was working at a restaurant again, waiting tables. It had been about two years since the drag shows, and they pretty much played out. There were no more bookings. Plus, I was getting tired of doing the shows. I needed to find something else to do that did not include wearing a girdle or pumps. I don't know how you girls do it! I knew I was not ready to start auditioning again—I just didn't have it in me. I decided to create my own work by writing. I considered different things about which I could write—maybe I could tell stories about humorous things that had happened to me. Lisa suggested that we write something together. She, too, had decided to stop auditioning. Misery loves company! We decided to write about the drag shows and all the funny things we encountered trying to set them up. We would change names and add a few fictitious characters and some humorous conflicts. It would all make for a great screenplay. For the following two months, all Lisa and I did was write during the day and work at night.

I remember how cold it was that fall. In fact, everyone I knew had gotten sick. My sister and the kids had the flu, which they passed on to the rest of us. Even Mamma, who never got sick, caught the bug. I was the first to come down with the flu in our house, so I was the first to feel better. One night when everyone was feeling better, I decided I would cook dinner for the family and give Mamma a break. Oh, but what to make? Then I remembered this great chicken dish Mamma use to make. It was actually my grandfather's recipe, but he passed away before I was born, so I never tasted the way he made it. It was fried chicken cutlets cooked in butter and oil and topped with this delicious wine and vegetable sauce. It turned out to be quite good. Mamma loved it. Said it tasted just like Grandpa's. "Couldn't have made it any better myself," she said. I guess a little bit of Mamma had rubbed off on me.

The fall went by quickly, and before we knew it, Christmas was only a couple of weeks away. Mamma was busy planning the menus for the holidays. My father had almost completed decorating the house. The Christmas tree was up and decorated. As they say, "It was beginning to look a lot like Christmas." Good grief, I never realized how corny I really am. One morning, about ten days before Christmas, I was working on my computer, and Mamma called me to help her in the kitchen. I should have known something was wrong, because she was moving around very slowly. At lunchtime, she called me again. I thought she had made something, and I was getting my tasting bowl. When I got downstairs, she was sitting in a chair and did not look well. I asked if she was okay. At that moment my whole life was about to change. She said, "I think you need to call 911." I hope you never have to go through such an experience. The time between the 911 call and the time the paramedics arrive feels like an eternity. Thankfully, my sister lived around the corner and was here within minutes. She called my mom at work. I helped Mamma to the couch and sat next to her, holding her hand. By this time the paramedics arrived, my sister had taken over. I just sat there holding Mamma's hand. She motioned for me to come closer. I remember this as if it were yesterday. I leaned down waiting to hear her tell me how much she loved me or that everything was going to be okay. Instead she just looked up at me and said, "You're a little heavy, and you're leaning on me." Then she smiled her special smile—the one I had seen all my life. I thought, "What would I do without her. How could I get through my life without her advice, her stories, her love?"

She died two days later. That Christmas was hard for us all. We were all going through the motions because of the kids. On Christmas Eve day, I decided to make a marinara sauce for that night. I thought of the stuffed squid that Mamma had planned to make. It was one of the traditional fish that she made on Christmas Eve, and I wished I knew how to make it. (Eventually, I did learn.) While the sauce was cooking, I went upstairs to shower. My mom was in her room. She came into the hallway looking for me oddly, because she was shocked that I was trying to make the stuffed calamari. I laughed and told her I wasn't. She said, "But I smell it." I took a whiff, and for a second so did I. I guess Mamma wanted us to know that she was there with us.

Chicken Cutlets With Vegetable Wine Sauce

Ingredients:
6 carrots (or more to taste)
6 celery stalks (or more to taste)
3 chicken bouillion
3 cups water
12 chicken legs, boned (drumstick and thigh) or 6 breasts, boned and cut in half
1 pound of mushrooms
1 stick plus 2 tablespoons butter
1 ½ cup of dry white wine
Breading for fried chicken
Olive oil and / or butter for frying
3 tablespoons of all-purpose flour
3 tablespoons of marsala

Dice carrots and celery into small pieces and boil in 3 cups of boullion for 3 minutes. Drain. Fry mushrooms, carrots, and celery in 2 tablespoons of butter until dry. Gradually add ½ cup of dry white wine. Set aside.

Bread and fry chicken cutlets – see page 104
Place fried chicken in a pan, in layers if necessary. Add ½ cup of dry white wine and steam for 5 minutes. This can be done 1 or 2 hours before serving.

When ready to serve: In a separate pan, heat remaining butter over a low flame. Remove pan from heat, add 3 tablespoons of flour, and brown. Let cool. While gently stirring, add remaining white wine and Marsala. Add this to the vegetables and mix well. Add vegetables to chicken and cook slowly for about 10 minutes or less. Keep checking so the chicken will not stick to the bottom of the pan. Serves 6.

Chicken Cutlets With Vegetable Wine Sauce

You Never Know When You're Making a Memory

Okay, back to Sunday dinner—the zucchini Parmigiana is in the oven. It's a great dish. Fried zucchini slices are layered with mozzarella, grated Parmigiano Reggiano cheese, and marinara sauce. I also made my low-fat recipe by baking the zucchini instead of frying them and by using low-fat cheese. My sister and I prefer the lower fat version. At this point in time, I am not just eating dietetically, but I am also controlling my portions, as Mamma had once suggested. I'm losing weight slowly, but this time I will keep it off. Yes, some days I do eat the original recipes, but I take very small portions. Everyone will be here in an hour for dinner, and I'm running late because Mass went into overtime. Yes, even though I'm the poster child for everything the church is against, I still go. The salad is made, and Mom is setting the table. As I look into the dinning room, for a second I imagine I see my grandmother there, too. For the moment, time has not moved on. Then I take a second look, and see my mom, and only my mom, setting the dining room table. While I watch her, sadness overcomes me. There are so many people who will be missing tonight for dinner. Mamma has been gone now for thirteen years, and my dad has been gone nine years. I just don't know where all the time went. I'm still living at home, which works out great. My mom's not alone, and I can keep an eye on her. I work part-time, which enables me to work on my writing. I'm able to go to L.A. when I need to go, and I always have a home base to which I can return. I still act, but I don't pursue acting as I did in the past. If a good part comes up, I'll do it. Lisa and I did write the screenplay about the drag shows. It's called "What A Drag." I'm trying to get it made into a movie. I also wrote a pilot about a gay uncle who is raising his three nieces and nephews called "Uncle Mom." I wrote and directed two short films that won honorable mention at several film festivals. Things are good. Oh, and if you're wondering if I'm dating, this Snow White is still waiting for his Prince Charming.

As we sit around the table enjoying dinner, I look at my family. My nephews are arguing with each other just as my brother and I used to do. As I watch my sister talking to my mom and sister-in law, I notice how much her hands are like Mamma's. My brother is sitting at the head of the table, joking with his daughters, reminding me of the way Dad joked around with my sister. Everyone is having a great time, enjoying being together. That's why I cook every Sunday, and that's why Mamma did it. When we are all together like this, I feel that Mamma is looking down and smiling. I also hope that when she does look down from heaven, and I have no doubt that's where she is, she knows how special she made all of our lives, and I hope she also realizes I am who I am because of what she taught me and because of how much she loved me.

Oh, and if you're wondering, yes, I am still fighting the battle of the bulge, but luckily, I've learned that it's okay to enjoy Mamma's original recipes as long as you use portion control. If you've overindulged and need to lose a few pounds, then you should go with my lower-fat versions. Don't worry, Mamma would approve of all of the recipes. Whichever you choose, cook and be with your family and friends; but most of all, make wonderful memories that will last a lifetime.

Mamma's Zucchini Parmigiana

Ingredients:
8 medium zucchini
1 or 2 eggs
1 cup of all-purpose flour
2 cups frying oil
Marinara sauce – see page 11
½ cup Parmigiano Reggiano
½ pound mozzarella cheese
Salt

Select firm zucchini, wash, and scrape lightly. Remove the top of the zucchini and cut a thin slice from the bottom. Cut the zucchini in half, then slice lengthwise into strips ¼-inch thick. Place on a rack to dry overnight, making sure that both sides are aerated. If you do not have a rack (or a screen), place the sliced zucchini on a tablecloth to dry, turning often. (When the zucchini are dried, they absorb less oil when fried and will not become soggy.)

To prepare:

Dip zucchini in beaten egg, salt, and flour. Fry in hot oil for about 3 minutes or until slightly brown, turning once. Drain on paper toweling.

Cover the bottom of a baking dish with a small amount of marinara sauce. Place a layer of zucchini over the sauce, sprinkle with Parmigiano Reggiano, add a layer of mozzarella, and cover with a ladleful of marinara sauce. Continue layering in this way, ending with zucchini. Cover with marinara sauce and sprinkle with Parmigiano Reggiano. Bake for 15 minutes in a moderate oven (350 degrees). Serves 8 to 10.

Greg's Reduced-Fat Zucchini Parmigiana

Ingredients:
8 medium zucchini
32-ounce container of low-fat Ricotta
1 cup low-fat Parmigiano Reggiano
Marinara sauce – see page 11
½ pound low-fat mozzarella cheese
Salt

Select firm zucchini, wash, and scrape lightly. Remove the top of the zucchini and cut a thin slice from the bottom. Cut the zucchini in half, then slice lengthwise into strips + 1/4-inch thick. Place on a rack to dry overnight, making sure that both sides are aerated. If you do not have a rack (or a screen), place the sliced zucchini on a tablecloth to dry, turning often. (When the zucchini are dried, they absorb less oil when fried and will not become soggy.)

To prepare:

Take zucchini and place on oven rack and bake at 375 degrees for 15 minutes. When finished, put aside.

In a large bowl, mix ricotta with ½ cup Parmigiano cheese and ½ cup of marinara sauce. Cover the bottom of a baking dish with a small amount of marinara sauce. Place a layer of zucchini over the sauce, then add a layer of the ricotta mixture and sprinkle with Parmigiano Reggiano; add a layer of mozzarella, and cover with a ladleful of marinara sauce. Continue layering in this way, ending with zucchini. Cover with marinara sauce and sprinkle with Parmigiano Reggiano. Bake for 15 minutes in a moderate oven (350 degrees).

Mamma's Zucchini Parmigiana

Mamma, Grandpa George and my Mom

Mom and Dad's Wedding 1957

One holiday dinner in 1968

Mamma as a young woman

Nana, Mom and Mamma 1957

A holiday with my two grandmothers

Just don't button it

Me and my Mom in 1965

Christmas dinner 1973

Me, my sister, brother and cousins

A Sunday at my Uncle's farm

All that jazz

Mamma cooking 1984

Camp Shane 1979 "Don't I look thrilled"

My sister, brother and me. So Stylish

Christmas
1985

Me and Mamma in Vegas

Time to make the donuts

Me and Steven at Dreamgirls

Me, Mamma and Paula 1988

My brothers wedding

Me as Jennifer Holiday

Me as Ethel Merman

Mamma and Aunt Idea 1994

Me, Mom and Mamma
after a show

Me with my nieces and
nephews

Me in a show in New York

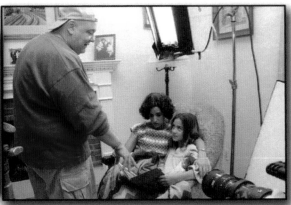

Me directing a short film I wrote

Mom and Mamma
in 1994

Me and Pam in
a show

My nephew Deniz's wedding

Other Great Family Recipes

Mom's Veal Scaloppini Cacciatore

Ingredients:
6 loin veal chops
½ cup flour
3 tablespoons olive oil
1 can of button mushrooms (or stems and pieces)
2 cloves garlic, chopped fine
1 cup of dry white wine
½ cup of canned plum tomatoes, chopped
Salt and pepper to taste
2 tablespoons chopped parsley

Dredge veal with flour. Heat olive oil in a heavy skillet and sauté meat until brown on both sides. Drain mushrooms (set liquid aside) and add to meat with the chopped garlic. Cover and simmer for 5 minutes. Add wine, tomatoes, and mushroom liquid. Season to taste with salt and pepper, cover, and simmer for about 15 minutes, or until meat is tender. Sprinkle steaks with chopped parsley and serve at once. Serves 6.

Mamma's Lamb Shanks

Ingredients:
4 meaty lamb shanks
2 cloves garlic, minced
1 large onion, chopped
½ cup of coarsely chopped celery
1 bay leaf
1 teaspoon dried oregano
1 cup tomato paste
½ cup red or white wine
Salt and pepper to taste
½ cup olive oil
2 cups water

In a covered roasting pan, combine all of the above ingredients. Bake for 1½ hours in a 350 degree oven. Uncover and bake for an additional hour, or until meat is very tender and sauce is thickened. Serve over rice. Serves 6.

Uncle Charlie's Marinated Salmon Topped With Greg's Mango Salsa

Ingredients:
1 cup soy sauce
½ cup cooking sherry
2 tablespoons sugar
4 cloves of garlic, sliced
6 large pieces of salmon fillet
1 diced jalapeno chili pepper
1 diced serrano chili pepper
3 medium fresh tomatoes, diced
½ chopped red onion, diced
1 peeled, diced mango
1 tablespoon fresh squeezed lime juice
½ cup chopped cilantro
½ teaspoon salt
¼ teaspoon pepper
1 teaspoon oregano

Uncle Charlie's Marinade:
Combine soy sauce, sherry, sugar, and garlic into a large pan. Mix well. Add the salmon to the marinade, cover, and marinate overnight.

Greg's Salsa:
Clean the chili peppers by removing the stems and seeds. Make sure you wear gloves or handle chili peppers with a fork. Wash your hands after handling and be sure not to touch your eyes for several hours, as the chilies are very hot and will irritate. Chop the tomatoes and chili peppers. Combine in a bowl with all the remaining ingredients.

Note: If you own a food processor, you can use it to mix everything but the mango, which will get too mushy. Mix mango in by hand. Chill for at least an hour.

Preparing the Salmon:
Place salmon in the broiler for 10 to 15 minutes. Serve topped with salsa. Serves 6.

Uncle Charlie's Marinated Salmon Topped With Greg's Mango Salsa

Mamma's Jambalaya

Ingredients:
¼ cup olive oil
1 onion, coarsely chopped
4 ribs of celery, coarsely chopped
1 clove garlic, minced fine
1 pepper (green or red), coarsely chopped
4 ripe tomatoes, blanched, peeled, chopped (or use 1 cup canned whole plum tomatoes, chopped)
1 (6-ounce) can tomato paste
Bay leaf and thyme, placed in a square of cheesecloth and tied
Tabasco to taste
3 cups water (or chicken broth)
1 cup Uncle Ben's Converted Rice
2 pounds shrimp
6 ounces of cooked ham, cubed

In a large pot, sauté in olive oil onion, celery, garlic, and pepper for 10 minutes. Add tomatoes, tomato paste, bay leaf and thyme pouch, Tabasco, and water (or broth). Cook about 10 minutes. Stir in rice, combining thoroughly. Cook until rice mixture is thick. Add shrimp and ham, and cook 10 to 15 minutes (until almost dry). Rice is usually cooked in about 20 minutes. Serve 4 to 6.

For a healthier choice you can use brown rice.

Mamma's Jambalaya

Nana's Spinach Turnovers

Ingredients:
Dough:
3 cups all-purpose flour, plus extra for flouring hands and board
½ teaspoon of salt
¼ teaspoon of pepper
⅓ cup oil (Wesson or Crisco) or ¼ pound of margarine
3 medium eggs or 2 large eggs
Warm water, beginning with 4 to 6 tablespoons

Make dough about 2 hours before you are ready to prepare the turnovers. You can make the dough by hand or in your mixer using dough hooks. If you are using a mixer, add the flour, salt, and pepper to the mixer bowl. Turn on the motor using a low speed. Add the oil, eggs, and a little water, gradually increasing the speed to work the dough. As you work the dough, sprinkle with water. When the dough becomes soft and elastic, take out of the mixer bowl and knead a few minutes more by hand until it is smooth like satin. It should be soft, smooth, and elastic. Cover the dough and let it rest for an hour.

If you are making the dough by hand, pour the flour onto your work surface to form a hill and make a well in the center, leaving some flour at the bottom of the well. Break the eggs into the center, add the oil, salt, pepper, and lightly scramble the eggs with a fork. With your hands, gradually pull flour in from the sides. Keep pushing up the flour on the outer wall of the well to keep the sides from breaking. Continue to do this until all the egg has been absorbed by the flour, forming a sticky dough. Sprinkle the work surface with flour and knead for 10 minutes. Do not let the dough get dry. If it appears too dry, slowly add drops of water to soften. The dough should be elastic but not sticky. As you knead, the dough will stick to your hands. Scrape your fingers and dust with a little flour before you start kneading again. The dough should be soft, smooth, and elastic. Cover the dough and let it rest for about an hour.

Filling:
2 onions, diced
2 bell peppers, diced
3 tablespoons of olive oil
½ a (28-ounce) can plum tomatoes, chopped
3 10-ounce packages frozen leaf spinach, cooked and well drained (squeeze out any excess water)

Sauté onions and peppers in olive oil. Add plum tomatoes and simmer until a little dry. Add spinach and mix well. Let cool.

Prepare Turnovers:
Roll out dough. Cut into 6-inch circles. Fold each circle in half just to make a crease in the middle. Unfold. You can now see the two halves (the top and the bottom half). Place some spoonfuls of the spinach filling on the bottom half of each circle, leaving ¼-inch border so the turnover can be crimped. When you are done, slightly wet the edge of the bottom half. Take the clean half (or top half) of the turnovers and fold over to cover the bottom half. Gently crimp the edge of the now semicircle with a fork to seal. Place turnovers on a greased cookie sheet. Bake at 350 degrees for 35 to 45 minutes, gently turning them over once with a large spatula so they will brown evenly. Yields 6 to 8.

Mamma's Stuffed Zucchini

Ingredients:
5 medium zucchini (10 if zucchini are small)
1 small onion
2 sprigs of parsley, chopped
4 slices of prosciutto, chopped
½ cup of bread crumbs
¼ cup grated Parmigiano Reggiano cheese
Salt to taste
½ cup butter (1 stick or 8 tablespoons)
3 tablespoons olive oil
Mozzarella cheese, cut in strips
2 eggs

Select firm zucchini, wash, and scrape lightly. Remove the top of the zucchini and quarter. Parboil in salted water. Remove from water with a slotted spoon and let cool. Scrape out center pulp and drain to remove all the water from the pulp. Hand squeeze if necessary. Set pulp aside.

Sauté onion in oil until golden. Add parsley and sauté a little longer. Add prosciutto, eggs, and zucchini pulp and mix well. Remove from heat and add bread crumbs and grated cheese. Mix well and cool. Salt each zucchini shell and stuff with filling. Grease a baking dish. Place stuffed zucchini side by side in the greased baking dish. Pour melted butter on top. Bake in a 350-degree oven for about 30 minutes. Place one strip of mozzarella cheese on each zucchini and put back in oven just long enough to melt cheese. Serves 10—two pieces per serving.

Grandpa George's Bows with Genoese Meat Sauce

Ingredients:
1 tablespoon butter
2 tablespoons olive oil
1 pound lean bottom round, cut into ½-inch cubes
1 teaspoon salt
2 medium onions, cut into eighths
1 clove garlic
½ cup dry white wine
1 teaspoon rosemary
1 can (10½ ounces) condensed beef consommé
1 can of water
1 tablespoon flour browned in 2 tablespoons of butter
1 box (12 ounces) egg pasta bows
Freshly grated Parmigiano Reggiano cheese

Heat butter and oil in a medium-size pot. Add meat, salt, onions, and garlic. Brown well, stirring occasionally. Remove garlic. Sprinkle meat with ¼ cup of wine and rosemary. Continue to cook a few minutes. Sprinkle with remaining wine. Cook a few minutes longer and remove from flame.

Combine consommé and water. Blend a small amount with browned flour and stir into meat. Add remaining consommé and water. Cover and simmer, stirring occasionally, until meat is tender, about 40-50 minutes.

When ready to serve, prepare egg bows as directed on package. Serve bows with meat sauce and top with grated cheese if desired. Serves 4.

Greg's Reduced-Fat Genoese Sauce

Ingredients:
Substitute reduced-fat margarine for butter
1 tablespoon of olive oil instead of 2
Use brown pasta

Continue with same directions as original recipe.

Mamma's Stuffed Mushrooms
Preheat oven to 375 degrees.

Ingredients:
20 large mushrooms and 2 cups chopped mushroom stems (amount will depend on how large mushrooms are)
1 stick butter
½ cup olive oil
1 finely chopped onion
2 cups chopped celery
¼ cup marsala wine
⅔ cup grated Parmigiano Reggiano
⅔ cup of seasoned bread crumbs
1 teaspoon salt
1 egg
Plus additional bread crumbs to top mushrooms.

Remove the stems from mushrooms and scoop out a small portion of each cap under the stem to make room for stuffing. Take stems and portion scooped from cap, chop, and put aside. Heat butter and oil in a large saucepan. Add chopped mushrooms, onions, and celery. Sauté for 7 to 8 minutes. Add marsala and cook for about 2 more minutes. Pour into a large mixing bowl and let cool for about 10 minutes. Once cooled, add cheese, bread crumbs, egg, and salt. Mix thoroughly. Fill each mushroom cap with stuffing. Use the palm of your hand to round the top and then dip stuffed top in breadcrumbs to seal. Place on a greased cookie sheet and bake at 375 degrees for 20 minutes. Serves 10.

Greg's Reduced-Fat Stuffed Mushrooms
Ingredients:
Replace 1 stick of butter with 4 teaspoons diet margarine
Replace ½ cup olive oil with 2 teaspoons olive oil
Use ½ cup vegetable broth when sautéing to keep moist
Use ⅔ cup reduced-fat grated Parmigiano Reggiano

Continue with same directions as original recipe.

Grandpa George's Bows with Genoese Meat Sauce

Mamma's Stuffed Mushrooms

Mamma's Meat Lasagne

Ingredients:
8 cups of Bolognese sauce – see page 32
1 pound of ricotta
Salt and pepper to taste
1 cup grated Parmigiano Reggiano cheese
1 egg
1 pound lasagne noodles
1 medium mozzarella, grated
Olive Oil Pam

Have Bolognese sauce already prepared and warm. Mix ricotta with ½ cup of sauce, salt, pepper, ½ cup of the grated Parmigiano, and egg. Cook lasagne in salted boiling water for 15 minutes or until tender. (Spray Olive Oil Pam in water to prevent sticking.) Drain and spread lasagne on a serving platter, spraying with Pam. Pour ½ cup of sauce on the bottom of a lasagne pan or dish sprayed with Olive Oil Pam. Put in a layer of lasagne, spread ricotta mixture over lasagne, add a layer of mozzarella and a ladle of sauce. Sprinkle with grated Parmigiano. Repeat layers until all ingredients are used, ending with a layer of lasagne covered with sauce. Bake in moderate oven (375 degrees) for 10 minutes or until lasagne is thoroughly heated. Serves 6.

Greg's Reduced-Fat Vegetarian Whole Wheat Lasagne

Ingredients:
8 cups marinara sauce – see page 11
2 cloves of garlic
1 tablespoon of olive oil
Olive Oil Pam
1 large bag of frozen chopped spinach (thawed with all water squeezed out)
1 pound of skim ricotta
Salt and pepper to taste
1 cup grated reduced-fat Parmigiano cheese
1 egg
1 pound of whole wheat lasagne
1 medium skim mozzarella, grated

Sauté garlic in olive oil in an Olive Oil Pam-sprayed pan until slightly browned. Add spinach and continue to sauté until spinach is cooked, about 10 minutes. Remove the two cloves of garlic and discard.

Have marinara sauce already prepared and warm. Mix ricotta with ½ cup of sauce, salt, pepper, ½ cup of the grated Parmigiano, and egg. Cook lasagne in salted boiling water for 15 minutes or until tender. (Spray Olive Oil Pam in water to prevent sticking.) Drain and spread lasagne on a serving platter, spraying with Pam. Pour ½ cup of sauce on the bottom of a lasagne pan or dish sprayed with Olive Oil Pam. Put in a layer of lasagne, spread ricotta mixture over lasagne, and add a thin layer of the sautéed spinach, a layer of mozzarella, and 1 cup of sauce. Sprinkle with grated Parmigiano. Repeat layers until all ingredients are used, ending with a layer of lasagne covered with sauce. Bake in moderate oven (375 degrees) for 10 minutes or until lasagne is thoroughly heated. Serve with remaining marinara sauce. Serves 6.

Nana's Stuffed Calamari (Squid)

Ingredients:
Marinara Sauce – see page 11
12 cleaned (thaw if frozen) calamari tubes about 4 inches long
  (if you buy fresh calamari, have them cleaned at fish store)
1 finely minced clove of garlic
1 cup white bread chopped in blender or crumbled by hand
2 tablespoons of Romano cheese
1 tablespoon olive oil
1 egg
¾ teaspoon of salt
¾ teaspoon of pepper
1 tablespoon parsley flakes

Combine all of the ingredients except calamari and sauce and mix well. Set aside.

Place calamari tubes in boiling water for about 1 minute until they open up. Drain well. Gently stuff each tube half full with prepared stuffing and close open end with a tooth pick. Place the calamari in the Marinara Sauce and simmer for 35 minutes. Gently remove the stuffed calamari from the sauce. Serve with linguine—two stuffed calamari tubes per serving. Serves 6.

Mamma's Mozzarella in Carrozza

Ingredients:
12 slices of white bread (I use Pepperidge Farm bread)
1 large mozzarella
3 eggs
½ teaspoon salt
½ cup all-purpose flour
2 cups of vegetable oil for frying (Crisco Oil is good)

Cut off crust from bread and cut in half. On six bread halves, place one slice of mozzarella approximately the same size as the bread and about ¼-inch thick. Top each with second bread half, making half a sandwich. Lightly beat eggs with salt. Dip the open edges of the half sandwiches into the flour to prevent the mozzarella from oozing out when fried. Dip half sandwiches into the egg and deep fry gently in hot oil, turning once so both sides are golden brown. Blot on a paper towel and serve immediately. Serves 6.

Greg's Brandy Shrimp Scampi

Ingredients:
1 stick of butter
¼ cup olive oil
6 cloves of chopped garlic
24 medium shrimp, cleaned and deveined (make sure shrimp is completely dry)
¼ cup chopped parsley
½ teaspoon of salt
½ teaspoon of black or red pepper
½ cup brandy or B&B liqueur

In a large skillet melt butter with olive oil. Sauté garlic for 5 minutes on a low flame. Add shrimp, parsley, salt, and pepper and sauté for 5 more minutes. Gradually add brandy and finish cooking for 5 more minutes, or until shrimp turn a beautiful shade of pinkish red. Serves 4.

Greg's Reduced-Fat Brandy Shrimp Scampi

Ingredients:

Substitute for sauce ½ cup of reduced-fat margarine instead of butter.
Use only 2 teaspoons of olive oil and add ¼ cup of chicken broth.

Continue with same directions as original recipe.

Mamma's Mozzarella in Carrozza

Greg's Brandy Shrimp Scampi

Mamma's Potato and Onion Frittata

Ingredients:
8 eggs
Salt and pepper to taste
3 tablespoons oil
2 medium onions, coarsely chopped
2 peeled potatoes, diced

Break the eggs in a bowl; season with salt and pepper, beat with a fork, and set aside. Heat the oil in a frying pan over medium heat. Add the onions, reduce heat to moderate, and cook until the onions become translucent. Do not brown. Remove onions from the pan with a slotted spoon and set aside. Sauté the diced potatoes in the same pan for about 10 minutes or until lightly browned. (Add more oil if necessary.) Add the onions to the potatoes and mix well. Pour the eggs on the potatoes and onions. Lift the potatoes and onions mixture up with a spatula so the eggs will run to the bottom. When the bottom of the frittata has browned and appears solid and the top is almost cooked, turn the frittata so the other side will brown.

Notes:
Use a 9-inch nonstick frying pan or a nonstick frittata pan set. The frittata set has two frying pans, one deeper than the other.

When using the frittata set, sauté in the deeper pan. Prepare the frittata as above. When you have poured the eggs over the potatoes and onions, cover with the shallow pan and cook until almost completely set, about 15 minutes. To cook the opposite side, flip both pans by grasping the handles together. The frittata should be moist, not dry. Serves 6 to 8.

You can use your imagination and use other fillings for your frittatas, such as zucchini or leftover pasta. It's actually a very good way to utilize any of your leftovers.

Mom's Zabaione
(A Great Italian Dessert)

Ingredients:
3 egg yolks
3 tablespoons sugar
6 tablespoons marsala wine
2 egg whites, beaten stiff
1 cup heavy cream, beaten stiff

In the top of a double boiler over hot (not boiling) water, combine the egg yolks, sugar, and marsala. Beat until foamy and slightly thickened. Remove from the water and continue to beat until cool.

Add the egg whites and the whipped cream. Blend in gently but thoroughly with a wire whisk. Pour into dessert dishes and chill overnight. Makes 6 servings.

Mom's Christmas Cookies

Birds' Nest Cookies

Ingredients:
1 cup soft butter or margarine
½ cup brown sugar, packed
2 egg yolks, unbeaten
½ teaspoon vanilla extract
¼ teaspoon salt
2 cups sifted all-purpose flour
2 egg whites, unbeaten
1¼ cups finely chopped walnuts
Raspberry jam

Start heating oven to 350 degrees. On medium speed of your electric mixer, cream butter until light and fluffy, gradually adding brown sugar. Add egg yolks and mix well. On low speed of your electric mixer, blend in vanilla, salt, and flour. Shape dough into 1-inch balls. Dip each ball in egg white, then nuts. On ungreased cookie sheets, place 1-inch apart. Bake 5 minutes. Remove from oven and, with the end of a wooden spoon, quickly make a depression in each cookie. Return to oven and bake 8 minutes longer. Cool. Fill depression with jam. Makes about 3½ dozen.

Mom's Christmas Cookies

Holiday Fruit Drops

Ingredients:
3½ cups sifted all-purpose flour
1 teaspoon baking soda
1 teaspoon salt
1 cup soft margarine
2 cups brown sugar, packed
2 unbeaten eggs
½ cup buttermilk, or 7 tablespoons milk mixed with 2 teaspoons white vinegar
1½ cups coarsely chopped pecans
2 cups halved candied cherries
2 cups cut-up pitted dates

Sift flour with baking soda and salt. On medium speed of your electric mixer, mix margarine, sugar, and eggs until creamy. On low speed of your electric mixer, blend in flour mixture alternating with buttermilk. Stir in pecans, cherries, and dates. Refrigerate at least one hour.

When ready to bake, preheat oven to 400 degrees. On greased cookie sheets, drop rounded tablespoonfuls of dough, 2 inches apart. Top each with a pecan half or half a candied cherry (or you may serve plain). Bake 8 to 10 minutes or until done. Makes 8 dozen.

Mom's Creamy Cheesecake

Crust ingredients:
1¾ cups graham cracker crumbs
¼ cup coarsely chopped walnuts
½ teaspoon of cinnamon
½ cup butter

Mix the above ingredients together. Use a 9-inch-by-3-inch round springform pan. Press crust ingredients to the bottom and three quarters of the way up the sides of the springform pan.

Filling ingredients:
3 well-beaten eggs
2 (8-ounce) packages of cream cheese (very soft)
1 cup sugar
¼ teaspoon salt
2 teaspoons vanilla
½ teaspoon almond extract
2 cups of sour cream

Combine all the ingredients for the filling except the sour cream and beat until smooth. Fold in the sour cream with a wire whisk. Pour filling into the crust and bake at 375 degrees for 35 minutes. (The filling will be soft when removed from oven but will solidify when chilled.) Let cool and refrigerate overnight. Serves 8 to 10.

Note: The cream cheese must be very soft before combining with other ingredients. If not, it will form tiny lumps that will not be melted by beating or baking.

Greg's Reduced-Fat Creamy Cheesecake

Ingredients
Substitute for crust ½ cup light margarine instead of butter
Substitute for filling 2 light or reduced-fat packages of cream cheese for regular
Substitute 2 cups of light sour cream for regular.

Continue with same directions as original recipe.

Creamy Cheesecake

Aunt Idea's Plum Cake

Ingredients:
¾ cup sugar
½ cup butter (or margarine)
1 cup unbleached all-purpose flour, sifted
1 teaspoon baking powder
Pinch of baking soda
¼ teaspoon salt
2 eggs
24 or more Italian purple plums, cut in half and pitted
Sugar, lemon juice, and cinnamon for topping

Preheat oven to 350 degrees.

Cream the sugar and butter in a good-size bowl. Add the flour, baking powder, baking soda, salt, and eggs. Beat well. Butter an 8 or 9 inch baking pan. Spoon batter into buttered baking pan and place plum halves skin side up over batter. Sprinkle with sugar, lemon juice, and a small amount of cinnamon. Bake for 1 hour at 350 degrees. Check occasionally to be sure it's not burning. Cool, then refrigerate or freeze if desired. (To serve frozen cake, reheat briefly at 300 degrees.) Serves 8 to 10.

Mamma's Paella

Ingredients:
1 pound Italian sausage
⅓ cup extra virgin olive oil
4 boneless chicken thighs, cut into medium chunks
4 boneless chicken breasts, cut into medium chunks
1 pound medium shrimp, shelled and deveined
4 lobster tails (6 to 8 ounces each), split
1 medium onion
8 garlic cloves (minced)
1 medium green bell pepper
1 medium red bell pepper
3 cups converted rice
3 cups chicken broth
2½ cups clam juice
2 bay leaves
1 teaspoon saffron
1 package (10 ounce) frozen peas, thawed
½ teaspoon salt
2 teaspoons black pepper
16 littleneck clams
16 small mussels
¼ cup fresh parsley
2 lemons, quartered

Prick the sausage all over with a fork. Place in a medium skillet with water to cover and bring to a simmer over moderately low heat; simmer for 10 minutes. Drain the sausage and slice into ½-inch rounds. In a large skillet, heat olive oil. Add cut-up chicken and sauté over moderately high heat, turning until browned all over and nearly cooked, about 10 minutes. Transfer chicken into a bowl. Add shrimp to the skillet and cook, tossing, for 30 seconds; remove with a slotted spoon. Add lobster tails and cook, turning occasionally, until the shells are red and the meat is slightly firm, about 6 minutes; remove with a slotted spoon.

Preheat oven to 350 degrees. Add the onion, garlic, and bell peppers to the skillet and cook over moderate heat until softened, about 5 minutes. Stir in the rice and cook, stirring, until translucent, about 4 minutes. Add the chicken broth, clam juice, bay leaves and the saffron. Bring to a boil, reduce the heat to low and cook, stirring occasionally, until rice is tender on the outside but still chewy in the center, about 10 minutes. Stir in the peas and salt and black pepper. Transfer the mixture to a 14-½-inch paella pan or a very large ovenproof skillet. Add the chicken and sausage. Bury shrimp, clams and mussels into the rice. Set the lobster tails on to the rice, flesh side down. Bake for 30 minutes, or until rice is tender and clams and mussels are opened. When you remove from the oven, cover with tin foil for 10 minutes. Sprinkle with parsley and garnish with lemons. Serves 10 to 12.

Greg's Chicken Pesto Over Pasta

Ingredients:
3 cups fresh basil leaves
⅓ cup pignoli nuts
4 small cloves of garlic
½ cup virgin olive oil (for pesto sauce)
1 cup grated Parmigiano Reggiano,
½ teaspoon of salt
½ teaspoon of pepper
2 tablespoons virgin olive oil (for sautéing)
4 boneless chicken breasts cut into 1-inch chunks
1 pound linguine

Pesto Sauce:
Combine the basil and the nuts and, using a food processor or a blender, pulse a few times to chop. Add garlic and pulse a few more times. Gradually add the ½ cup of olive oil while still pulsing. Stop and scrape sides with rubber spatula if needed. Add ½ cup grated cheese, salt and pepper and pulse a few more times until fully mixed. Set aside.

Pesto Chicken:
In a large skillet heat 2 tablespoons of olive oil and sauté chicken pieces for about 8 to 10 minutes. Lower heat. Slowly add the pesto sauce while constantly stirring. Cook over low heat for 5 minutes. Set aside, keeping warm.

Cook linguine al dente, drain, and transfer to a large bowl. Pour chicken pesto over cooked pasta. Toss, sprinkle with remaining Parmigiano Reggiano, and serve. Serves 4.

Greg's Chicken Pesto Over Pasta

Greg's Easy Swedish Meatballs

Ingredients:
Olive Oil Pam
2½ pounds of chopped meat loaf mix (beef, pork, veal)
4 cans of regular Campbell's Golden Mushroom Soup
1 egg, beaten
3 tablespoons of Worcestershire sauce
2 cups seasoned bread crumbs
Salt to taste
1 can of Campbell's Healthy Choice Cream of Mushroom Soup
2 cups of half-and-half

Spray a baking pan with Olive Oil Pam. In a large bowl, mix the ground meat, 1 can of Campbell's Golden Mushroom Soup, egg, 1 tablespoon of Worcestershire sauce, and the seasoned bread crumbs. Salt to taste. Shape into small meatballs—about 1-inch in diameter. Place the meatballs on the Pam-sprayed baking pan and bake at 350 degrees for 15 minutes or until browned. Check occasionally to prevent overbrowning.

Make the sauce while the meatballs are baking. In a medium pot, combine 1 can of Campbell's

Healthy Choice Cream of Mushroom Soup, 3 cans of Campbell's regular Golden Mushroom Soup, 2 tablespoons of Worcestershire sauce, and 2 cups of half-and-half. Heat to boiling, then simmer for about 10 minutes, stirring occasionally. Drop the baked meatballs into the sauce and continue to simmer for 10 additional minutes. Stir often to prevent sticking. If you feel the sauce is getting too thick, add a little more of the half-and-half. Serve hot in a chafing dish or in a large bowl.

To make a meat loaf:
Mix the meatball ingredients as above and shape into a loaf, or two smaller loaves if you so desire. Bake at 350 degrees for 40 minutes or until cooked. Make the sauce as above and pour over the meat loaf when serving.

Greg's Easy Reduced-Fat Swedish Meatballs

Ingredients:

Substitute ground turkey for meatloaf mix.
Substitute 2 cups of fat-free half-and-half for regular.

Continue with same directions as original recipes

Greg's Easy Swedish Meatballs

Mamma's Escarole Meatball Soup With Strufole

Chicken Soup – see page 60

Meatballs

Ingredients:
½ pound meat loaf mix (ground beef, veal and pork)
2 tablespoons fresh parsley
¼ cup grated Parmigiano Reggiano
½ cup bread crumbs
¼ teaspoon pepper
3 cloves of garlic, minced

In a large bowl, mix all ingredients by hand using a light touch. When fully mixed, grab small amounts of the mixture and roll into balls about the size of a marble, ½ inch in diameter. In a small pot heat about two cups of soup. Cook a few meatballs at a time in the soup for about 5 minutes. Soup should just cover the meatballs. When finished, put meatballs aside. Discard the soup.

Note: To make the meatballs lower fat, you can use veal or turkey instead of the beef and pork. Use low-fat cheese.

Mamma's Strufoli for Soup

Ingredients:
2 cups flour
¼ teaspoon salt
1 teaspoon baking powder
1 tablespoon Crisco shortening
3 large eggs, slightly beaten
Oil for frying (I use Crisco Oil)

Sift the flour, salt, and baking powder into a large bowl. Cut in Crisco as you would for a pie crust. Add the eggs and, with a wooden spoon, mix into a soft dough. Place dough on a lightly floured pastry board and knead for 8 minutes or until no longer sticky. The dough should be smooth and firm.

Divide the dough into 8 pieces and roll each piece into a rope ½ inch in diameter. Cut the ropes diagonally into pieces the size of a hazelnut, about ¼-inch long.

Heat about 3 inches of frying oil in a deep frying pan to 375 degrees on a deep fat thermometer. Fry the strufoli a few at a time until golden, turning them constantly with a wooden spoon to keep the strufoli separated. Using a slotted spoon, remove the fried strufoli, letting any excess oil drain back into the frying pan, and then drain on paper towels.

When the strufoli are cooled, store in a plastic container lined with paper toweling until ready to use. Will store well for one or two days.

Mamma's Lentil Soup

Ingredients:
¼ cup of olive oil
2 finely chopped cloves of garlic
1 cup medium chopped onions
1 cup medium chopped carrots
1 cup medium chopped celerys
4 ounces diced salt pork
2 cups crushed tomatoes (canned or fresh)
¼ cup of chopped parsley
1 pound rinsed lentil beans
3 quarts water
2 teaspoons salt
Dash of pepper

Heat oil in large pot over medium heat. Once oil is hot, sauté garlic, onions, carrots, and celery for approximately 7 to 8 minutes. Add salt pork, tomatoes, parsley, lentils, water, salt, and pepper. Reduce heat, cover, and cook for 45 to 50 minutes or until lentils are tender. Stir occasionally. Serves 6 to 8.

Greg's Vegetarian Fat-Free Lentil Soup

Ingredients:
3 quarts vegetable broth
2 finely chopped cloves of garlic
1 cup medium chopped onions
1 cup medium chopped carrots
1 cup medium chopped celerys
1 cup thawed, drained frozen spinach
3 cups crushed tomatoes (canned or fresh)
¼ cup of chopped parsley
1 pound rinsed lentil beans
2 teaspoons salt
Dash of pepper

Heat 1 cup of broth over medium heat. Once broth is hot, sauté garlic, onions, carrots, and celery for approximately 7 to 8 minutes. Add tomatoes, parsley, lentils, spinach, remaining broth, salt, and pepper. Reduce heat, cover, and cook for 45 to 50 minutes or until lentils are tender. Stir occasionally. Serves 6 to 8.

Mamma's Tiramisu

Ingredients:
3 egg yolks
¼ cup of caster or superfine sugar
1 teaspoon of vanilla extract
8 ounces of mascarpone cheese
1 pint (2 cups) of heavy cream, whipped
1½ cups of strong fresh coffee, cooled
2 tablespoons of rum
2 tablespoons of Kahlua
2 tablespoons of Tia Maria
12 ladyfingers
3 tablespoons of sifted cocoa powder or 4 ounces of shaved semisweet chocolate

Using a whisk or handheld mixer, whisk the egg yolks, sugar, and vanilla together in the top of a double boiler over gently simmering water. When thick and creamy, remove from the heat and cool. When cooled, beat in the mascarpone cheese. Fold in the whipped cream and set mixture aside.

Mix the coffee with the rum, Kahlua, and Tia Maria. Using a pastry brush, gently brush the ladyfingers with the coffee mixture. Layer the ladyfingers in a serving bowl or glass baking dish, and spread with half the mascarpone cheese and cream mixture. Repeat with another layer of the lady fingers and the remaining half of the mascarpone and cream mixture. Sprinkle with the cocoa powder or the shaved chocolate. Cover and refrigerate overnight or for at least 6 hours. Serves 6 to 8

Mamma's Tiramisu

Mamma's Eggplant Caponata

Ingredients:
1 medium-size eggplant
6 tablespoons olive oil
1 sliced onion
3 tablespoons Hunt's tomato sauce
2 stalks of celery, diced
1 tablespoon capers
4 green olives, coarsely chopped
2 tablespoons wine vinegar
1 tablespoon sugar
Salt and pepper to taste

The day before serving, peel eggplant and dice. Dry diced eggplant overnight on a flat, covered surface. (You can use an old tablecloth or some old dish towels for a cover.)

The next day, fry the eggplant in 6 tablespoons of olive oil for 6 to 8 minutes over medium flame. Remove eggplants from the pan and set aside. Brown onion in oil for 3 to 4 minutes. (If oil appears to be dried up, add one or two additional tablespoons.) Add Hunt's tomato sauce and celery and cook until celery is tender. If necessary, add a tablespoon of water. Return the eggplants to the pan and add the capers and chopped olives. Heat the vinegar and sugar and pour over eggplant. Season with salt and pepper to taste and simmer for about 10 minutes, stirring often. Cool. Serve with crackers or toasted bread squares. Refrigerates well for several days.

Mamma's Eggplant Caponata

Mamma's Foolproof Pie Crust Recipe
Recipe for Two-Crust Pie

Ingredients:
3 cups of sifted all-purpose flour
½ teaspoon salt
1½ cups of Crisco shortening
¾ cups cold water
Milk to brush on crust

Sift flour and salt together. Add half of the Crisco to flour. Cut in with pastry blender until mixture looks like meal. Add remaining Crisco and continue cutting until particles are the size of a navy bean. Sprinkle water 1 tablespoon at a time over mixture. With a fork, work lightly together until all particles are moistened and in small lumps. Add just enough water to moisten. (You may use all the water if necessary.) Press dampened particles together into a ball. Dough will be sticky. Do not be afraid to handle this dough or flour your hands while handling. Unlike other pie crust recipes, this dough will not spoil by overhandling. Wrap in wax paper and refrigerate for a half hour. (It is not necessary to refrigerate this dough, but it does make it easier to handle.)

To roll out dough:
Cut dough in two pieces, making one piece (bottom crust) slightly larger than the other. Shape pieces into balls. Roll out bottom crust on a floured board to 1/8-inch thickness. Roll dough from center to edges in all directions to make an even circle. Make circle 2 inches larger all around than the pie plate. When rolling out dough, use as much flour as necessary. It won't spoil this dough. To transfer dough to pie plate, roll the dough circle onto the rolling pin and carefully unroll into the pie plate. (Or fold dough circle in half and lift into pie plate. Unfold and fit into bottom and sides of pie plate.) Add filling. Roll top crust as directed above for the bottom crust and center over filling. With scissors, trim pastry edges, leaving a 1-inch overhang. Fold overhang under, then bring up over pie-plate rim. Crimp edges with fingers to build an attractive rim for pastry. Brush top crust lightly with milk (but not the edges). Prick top crust in several places with a fork. Bake according to pie recipe.

Note:
You can roll out the dough between two pieces of wax paper. Center a 12-inch square of wax paper on pastry board. Lightly flour the paper and place dough in center. Lightly flour dough and cover with a second 12-inch square of waxed paper. Roll out as described above. Gently peel off the top piece of wax paper. Fold remaining wax paper with dough in half. Carefully lift into pie plate. Gently peel off waxed paper and guide into bottom and sides of plate. Do the same for the top crust.

For Single-Crust Pie

Use half of the ingredients for the two-crust pie recipe. Roll dough as directed.

For a Baked Pie Crust Shell

Some recipes call for a baked pie crust shell. Use half of the two-crust pie recipe. Roll out the dough on a lightly floured board 1/8-inch thick as directed above. Fit it into an 8- or 9-inch pie plate. Prick bottom and sides of pastry with a fork. Set a pie pan filled with dried beans on the dough, weighing it down. Bake in a hot oven, 450 degrees, on the center rack, for 12 minutes. Remove the top pie pan filled with dried beans and brown the crust 5 minutes more, if necessary.

Mom's Blueberry Pie

Ingredients:
1 quart blueberries
2½ tablespoons quick-cooking tapioca
⅔ cup granulated sugar
¼ teaspoon salt
1 tablespoon lemon juice (or vinegar)
1 recipe for two-crust pie – see page 98
½ cup brown sugar firmly packed
1 tablespoon butter

Wash the blueberries and remove any small stems. Drain well. Dry gently with paper towel if necessary. Mix blueberries, tapioca, granulated sugar, salt, and lemon juice, and let stand while making the pie crust.

For piecrust, follow the directions for Mama's Foolproof Pie Crust Recipe – see page 98
Roll dough as directed. Line a 9-inch pie plate. Fill shell with berry mixture. Sprinkle with brown sugar, and dot with butter. Center top crust directly over filling and seal edge of pie as directed in pie crust recipe. Bake in 425-degree oven for 30 to 40 minutes. Serves 8 to 12.

Aunt Nina's Swedish Apple Cake

Ingredients:
Cake:
1½ cups sifted all-purpose flour
1 teaspoon of sugar
½ cup butter, softened
1 egg yolk
2 tablespoons milk
4 cups sliced apples

In a medium mixing bowl, sift together flour and sugar. Work in butter until well blended. Stir in egg yolk beaten with milk. Line an 8- or 9-inch cake pan or pie pan with mixture and cover with sliced apples arranged in a circular pattern. Cover apples with the following topping.

Topping:
Mix the following ingredients well and spread over fruit.

¾ cup sugar
1½ tablespoons all-purpose flour
2 tablespoons butter
¼ teaspoon salt
1 teaspoon vanilla extract

Bake in preheated 400-degree oven for 1 hour. Watch towards the end of the cooking time not to burn the crust. Serves 8.

Mom's Pumpkin Pie

Ingredients:
1½ cups pumpkin (one 15-ounce can)
¾ cup sugar
1¼ cups of whole milk or evaporated milk
2 tablespoons of molasses
1 egg, slightly beaten
1 tablespoon cornstarch
½ teaspoon salt
1 teaspoon cinnamon
¼ teaspoon ginger
¼ teaspoon nutmeg
1 recipe for single-crust pie – see page 98

Stir pumpkin and sugar together and heat until hot. Add the milk and molasses that have been heated. Combine the balance of the ingredients and add. Stir to mix well. Pour into an unbaked 8- or 9-inch pie crust – see page 98

Bake in a preheated oven at 425 degrees for 20 minutes. Reset the temperature to 325 degrees and bake 35 minutes longer. Serves 8 to 12.

Serve with whipped cream topping.

Mom's Pumpkin Pie

Shrimp and Mushrooms Fra Diavolo Over Pasta

Ingredients:
4 tablespoons of olive oil
1 clove of elephant garlic, coarsely chopped
1 teaspoon of crushed red pepper
1 (28-ounce size) can of crushed tomatoes
1 cup of sliced oyster mushrooms
1 cup of sliced portabella mushrooms
1 cup of sliced white mushrooms
1 small jar (no more than 8 ounces) of sun-dried tomatoes, drained and rinsed
½ cup of clam juice
Salt to taste
1½ pounds of shrimp, peeled and deveined
1 pound of cooked pasta

Heat olive oil over medium flame for 1 or 2 minutes. Sauté the garlic and the crushed red pepper in the olive oil until garlic is lightly browned. Add the crushed tomatoes, mushrooms, sun-dried tomatoes, and clam juice. Salt to taste. Cook for 15 minutes on medium heat. Add the shrimp. Cook for an additional 10 minutes. Serve over pasta. Serves 6 to 8.

Reduced-Fat Fra Diavolo
Spray a medium pot with Olive Oil Pam. Reduce the oil to 2 tablespoons.

Serve over whole wheat pasta.

Shrimp and Mushrooms Fra Diavolo Over Pasta

Nana's Rice Sattu (Casserole)

Ingredients:
1 cup rice (I use Uncle Ben's Converted Rice)
½ stick of butter (4 tablespoons), melted
4 eggs, slightly beaten
1 cup grated Parmigiano Reggiano
1 cup diced mozzarella cheese
1½ cups ricotta cheese
Salt and pepper to taste
1 tablespoon of chopped parsley
Marinara sauce – see page 11

Boil rice until firm and drain well. In a bowl, mix cooked rice, melted butter, and eggs. Add the grated cheese, mozzarella, ricotta, salt and pepper to taste, and chopped parsley. (If you have any leftovers you wish to use up, you may dice and add to mixture.) Butter a baking dish and flour. Add mixture to baking dish, dot with butter, and bake at 350 degrees for a half hour. Serve with marinara. Serves 6.

Mamma's Osso Buco

Ingredients:
6 veal shin bones (should be meaty and about 4 inches long)
All-purpose flour
½ cup butter (1 stick)
Chopped mixture of:
  1 carrot
  1 stalk of celery
  1 onion
  1 clove garlic (chopped fine)
  1 teaspoon dried marjoram
Salt and pepper to taste
½ cup of dry white wine
4 ripe tomatoes, blanched, peeled, chopped (or 1 cup canned whole plum tomatoes chopped)
1½ cups of beef stock
1 clove garlic, chopped fine
1 teaspoon grated orange rind (no white part)
1 teaspoon grated lemon rind (no white part)

Roll the shin bones in flour. Heat 4 tablespoons of the butter in a heavy pot over fairly high heat until golden. Brown the veal shin bones on all sides in the butter. Remove from pot and set aside.

Add the chopped mixture to the pot, season with salt and pepper, and stir for a minute or two to mix well. Add the white wine and cook until it has evaporated. Return the veal shin bones to the pot, placing upright to prevent the marrow from falling out. Add the tomatoes and stock and bring to a boil. Reduce the heat and simmer in covered pot for about 1 hour, checking occasionally. About 10 minutes before the meat on the shin bones is fully cooked and tender, remove the lid, raise the heat, and reduce the sauce slightly. Remove the bones and place on a heated serving platter. Add the remaining butter, chopped garlic, and grated orange and lemon rind to the sauce and cook for a minute or two. Cover the veal shin bones with the sauce. Serves 6.

Mamma's Osso Buco

Fried Chicken Cutlets

Ingredients
12 thin sliced chicken breasts or thighs
3 cups seasoned breadcrumbs
4 slightly beaten eggs
1 to 3 cups of frying oil depending on size of skillet

Dip chicken breasts or thighs into beaten eggs then roll in breadcrumbs, completely coating chicken. Layer coated chicken breast on a platter, separating layers with wax paper.

Heat oil in a large skillet. Fry cutlets over medium flame, a few at a time, for 4 to 6 minutes or until golden brown on both sides. Drain fried cutlets on paper toweling to remove excess oil.

Place on a platter and serve immediately with wedges of lemon. Serves 6.

Fried Chicken Cutlets

Index

For info or comments write to:

Gregory Gallerano
c/o GLG Productions
PO Box 125
Essex Fells, NJ 07021
or
E-mail Greg at:
glg2611@gmail.com

Visit us online:

www.itsneverjustthefood.com